Prologue

Luis Bridger lay staring at the ceiling of the utilitarian hotel room. "I don't think I've ever been this happy."

Jordan rolled toward him and snuggled close. "It's been an incredible three days."

"Sure has." He stroked her golden hair. "I expected the clinic to be awesome. I didn't expect you."

"Ditto, cowboy. I've been to several of these. Never had this kind of extracurricular fun."

"Several? I don't think I knew that. No wonder you were the star pupil."

"I'd better be if I want to take my show on the road next spring."

"About that." He loved sliding his fingers through her silky hair. Loved stroking her satin skin. Her body thrilled him. He didn't want the fun times to end. "Do you have a plan?"

"Absolutely. I'm working two jobs this winter to build up my savings while I set up my clinic schedule for next year."

"Any chance you and Fudge will be in my neck of the woods?"

"Um… maybe, but…."

Her hesitation said it all. "Hey, forget I asked." He shouldn't have. They'd agreed not to pursue a relationship. They hadn't exchanged phone numbers. No calls. No texts.

"It's okay." Her warm breath tickled his skin. "I'll be sad to say goodbye, too. But I need to pour all my energy into making this work."

"I get it. I just hate to think we'll never see each other again. That we'll completely lose touch."

"If you send a postcard to my P.O. box, I'll write back. Maybe not immediately, but...."

"Okay." A postcard. *How are you? I am fine. XO, Luis.* Not happening. "And you can always find me at Laughing Creek Ranch."

Changing her position, she lifted her head and met his gaze, her blue eyes filled with tenderness. "I won't forget you."

"I won't forget you, either." He pushed away the sadness and cupped her cheek. "Checkout isn't until eleven. We don't have to say goodbye, yet, *querida.*"

"No." She smiled. "No, we don't." Leaning closer, she kissed him.

With a soft groan he abandoned himself to the lure of her kiss. One last time.

WHEN A COWBOY TEMPTS FATE

THE BRIDGER BUNCH

Vicki Lewis Thompson

Ocean Dance Press

WHEN A COWBOY TEMPTS FATE
© 2025 Vicki Lewis Thompson

ISBN: 978-1-63803-899-3

Ocean Dance Press LLC
PO Box 69901
Oro Valley, AZ 85737

This is a work of fiction. Any resemblance to
actual persons, living or dead, business
establishments, events, or locales is entirely
coincidental.

Visit the author's website at
VickiLewisThompson.com

1

Looks like we might see each other over Fourth of July weekend!

Jordan Sterling's cheery email played in a loop in his head. She'd likely staked out a spot along the parade route, eager to experience the Mustang Valley festivities Luis had raved about five years ago. And he still hadn't told his family squat about her. *Way to dig yourself a hole, idiot.*

"You're muttering to yourself, *hermano.*" His brother Xavier gazed across the golden rumps of Woody and Buzz, the palominos hitched to the Hearts & Hooves wagon promoting the wild horse sanctuary. "Something wrong?"

"Not a thing, Zay." He adjusted the traces on his side, fighting the urge to glance around for any sign of Jordan in the crowded parade staging area.

"Parade jitters?"

"Nah. We've got this." He glanced in the back of the wagon where his sister Claudette had been organizing the logo hats and T-shirts she'd toss to the crowd along the way. The new digital adoption program allowed them to be generous with merch. "Where's Claudie?"

"She forgot the T-shirt cannon. She went to fetch it from her truck. She's been gone a while. Probably got involved in a conversation."

"It happens." He hadn't noticed she'd left until now. Time to get his head out of his butt. "You'd better start unloading the rest of the horses from the trailer. I'll help once she gets back. We don't want to leave this creation of yours unattended."

"I appreciate that. It's more fragile than it looks. How about I locate Rio and send him over to babysit the wagon?"

"Sounds good." Their youngest brother sometimes had trouble focusing, but he'd probably do a better job than he was managing right now.

After Zay went in search of Rio, Luis stepped back from the wagon and admired Zay's masterpiece. He'd turned the H&H logo into a life-sized wire sculpture of a running mustang. Filled out with black carnations for the coat and long grasses for a flowing mane and tail, it was so lifelike he expected it to start breathing.

The high school parking lot was full of kids who'd love to climb on that horse. He'd discouraged several already. Normally the staging area chaos energized him — horses whinnying, dogs barking, old friends calling out to each other and the marching band's drumline maintaining a steady rat-a-tat-tat.

He tried to blame his anxiety on his new responsibilities. He'd taken over organizing the Laughing Creek entry from his brother Adam, who now had mayoral duties including serving as parade marshal with his new bride Tracy.

But it wasn't that. He was good with added responsibility. Always had been.

Moving to the head of the matched team, he gave Woody and Buzz head scratches and nose rubs. "I can't stop thinking about her, guys."

Woody shoved his nose into the palm of his hand, a clear sign of support.

"And I don't know how to explain to my family about her if they see us together."

Both geldings eyed him with such forbearance that he laughed. "I know. I'm being dramatic. When I saw her name on the list of digital adopters four months ago, I could've said *Oh, by the way, I know her. We met at a clinic five years ago.*"

Buzz rumbled a comment.

"But I didn't expect to see her ever again, so I let it go." He combed his fingers through the palominos' silky forelocks and their eyelids drifted to half-mast. He envied them their relaxation.

"Now she's signed up for the H&H tour this weekend."

Woody let out a horsy sigh.

"No kidding. We're guaranteed to see each other. And I have no idea what—"

"Hey, *hermano*, guess what?" Rio arrived looking pleased with himself. "Sophie asked me to go with her to the laser show tonight."

"I'm shocked." The first kid born to the blended family, Rio had inherited their dad's blue eyes and their mom's dark wavy hair that matched Luis's.

Both their parents had predicted the kid would be a hit with the ladies and they hadn't been wrong. At twenty-four he'd already turned down two marriage proposals.

His cocky grin softened and the sparkle faded from his eyes. "Do you suppose anybody but us remembers Dad was the one who talked the town council into a laser show instead of fireworks?"

"The old-timers on the council do. The wild herds hated those fireworks."

"And Dad. He despised them." Rio shoved his hands in his pockets. "Days like today, I really miss him."

"Same here." He gave Rio's shoulder a squeeze. "Watch the wagon for me, okay? Make sure kids don't try to get up on it. I'm gonna help Zay unload. Claudie should be here soon."

"When she gets here, I'll come help you. I meant to do that with these two." He motioned to Woody and Buzz. "But then Sophie called me over and I—"

"No worries. We managed. See you soon." He shoved away thoughts of Jordan and concentrated on the work ahead.

The pace picked up as the start time grew closer. Betty Jamison, a ninety-two-year-old member of the town council and the only parade chairperson he had ever known barked out the ten-minute warning on her megaphone.

Mounted on Scout, his butterscotch and white pinto, he kept on the move checking to make sure nobody had an issue. Claudie was back on the H&H wagon with the t-shirt cannon and Mila had climbed into the driver's box. They'd be leading the Bridger Bunch entry.

Behind them, his mom drove the team pulling the flatbed that featured a patriotic theme. In the past, Grandma Doris and the aunties had been satisfied with red, white and blue outfits, some bunting and a stash of candy they tossed to the kids.

But this year they'd leveled up, going public with their Dazzling Damsels nickname. Auntie Kat had commissioned Zay to create two sparkly banners, which he'd mounted on either side of the flatbed's low railing. And the Damsels had created costumes.

Draped in silver satin with a torch and a silver crown, Auntie Kat portrayed the Statue of Liberty. Because the material tended to slip, and Auntie Kat was a former model, Lady Liberty wore a flag-themed bikini underneath. Grandma Doris had opted to be Betsy Ross in a ruffled cap and a Revolutionary-era gown sitting in a rocker with a ginormous flag in her lap.

Auntie Carmen's suffragette outfit was a long white dress and a wide-brimmed straw hat. Her protest sign read *We are the 51% minority.* Auntie Ezzie had tricked herself out as Rosie the Riveter and held a sign that said *We can do it!* She'd been lifting weights for two months so she'd have biceps to show off.

Luis paused next to the flatbed and give them all two thumbs up. "Lookin' good!"

"Check this out." Auntie Ezzie came over to his side of the flatbed, flexed her arm and produced a small bulge.

He knew better than to laugh. "Whoa! *Muy bueno, tia.*"

She grinned. "Wanna arm wrestle?"

"It's a date. After the parade."

"Places, everyone! Places!" Betty's voice blared from her megaphone. A former first-grade teacher, she corralled the participants with the same no-nonsense method that worked for six-year-olds. "We step off in two minutes!"

Nudging Scout into a trot, he joined his four siblings gathered on horseback behind the flatbed. "Everybody ready?"

"I can't wait." Greta, his youngest sister, had worn her blinged-out jeans and shirt, her best hat and her fanciest boots. Her golden hair glinted in the sun.

"You're beautiful. So's Muffin."

"It took forever, but it was worth it." She'd braided ribbons and flowers into her buckskin's mane and tail.

He glanced at Monty, Zay and Rio. "You guys clean up pretty good, too."

"Better than last year," Monty said.

"Yeah, well...." The last July Fourth had been the first one without their dad. They'd struggled to make an effort. "He'd be proud of us today."

"Gotta make Adam proud, too," Zay said. "The mayor's family can't show up looking like bums."

Greta sighed. "I *am* proud of him, but it feels weird that he's up front instead of back here with us."

"At least he and Tracy insisted on riding Banjo and Moonlight instead of cruising along in somebody's ragtop doing the royal wave." Rio made a face. "That's so not Bridger Bunch style. We—"

"And we're rolling!" Betty called out and the band struck up *Stars and Stripes Forever.*

"Show time." Zay tilted his head toward Rio and the two wheeled their horses in behind Greta.

Also riding abreast, Luis and Monty took the rear so they could monitor everything ahead of them. Since Laughing Creek Ranch's entry was in the middle of the procession, they were in sight of the square within a few minutes.

"You did great, bro." Monty raised his voice to be heard over the band. "I can tell you're stressed, but you should be able to relax, now. The hardest part's over."

"Maybe." The sun beat down on him, which explained why he was sweating. It wasn't the thought of seeing Jordan. "It's a parade, though. Things can still go sideways."

"The weather's gorgeous so let's think positive."

"Alrighty." If he kept his gaze unfocused, he might not notice her in the crush of folks on the sidewalk. That was probably the smart move. No telling how he'd react if he saw her.

Then again, he might not even recognize her. She could have changed her hair color, put on weight, lost weight. Five years was a lot. People changed. She could look totally—

Beautiful. The breath left his lungs. She was here, unmistakable in the crowd gathered in front of the Golden Nugget. She hadn't worn a hat and her blonde hair shone bright even in the shade.

Yearnings he would have sworn he'd ditched years ago swept through him.

She hadn't spotted him yet. She was too enthralled by the show happening on the flatbed.

He should stop looking at her. But she drew him like a magnet, exactly the way she had five years ago. Had he known this might happen?

Yes, dammit. On some level he'd suspected the fire still burned. No wonder he'd avoided mentioning Jordan to his family, to *anyone*. He'd known it would provide oxygen to the simmering coals.

Was that true for her? Is that why she'd come to the parade and signed up for the tour? He'd done a good sales job on his family and the wild horse sanctuary, but maybe she was here because of *him*.

In which case he needed to figure out what he wanted to do about it.

<u>2</u>

Jordan eased carefully out the revolving door of the Golden Nugget Hotel, her small backpack over one shoulder. Folks sat elbow-to-elbow in camp chairs while they chattered like a flock of sparrows. Kids took turns sitting on the curb or dashing into the street to see if the parade was coming.

The historic three-story hotel provided a lot of shady sidewalk, making it prime real estate for parade watching. She had no place to stand without blocking the hotel's entrance.

Two sixty-something men sporting identical handlebar mustaches leaned against the building along with several others without chairs. Motioning to her, they made room for her between them.

"Thanks." She squeezed in and cradled the backpack in front of her. Both men had clearly applied plenty of shaving lotion this morning. A little overwhelming, but she was grateful for their hospitality.

"Visiting?" asked the one on her left. The logo for the barbershop next door featured a handlebar mustache. She had a hunch that was no coincidence.

"Yes, I'm visiting. My name's Jordan."

"Pleased to meet you, Miss Jordan. I'm Marv and he's Harry. We—"

"Let me guess. You own Shear Thing, the place next door."

Marv's eyes twinkled. "Smart lady."

"You're the smart ones, branding yourselves with those awesome 'staches."

Harry laughed. "It's corny, but our customers love it, just like they love that twirling barber pole out front. Nostalgia works in this town."

"I'll bet. How come you're not watching from the front of your shop?"

"We were planning on it." Marv glanced in that direction. "Then customers arrived with two ratty camp chairs that looked ready to collapse, so we set them up in our chairs and moved down here."

"That was nice of you."

"Our customers are like family," Harry said. "What's your specialty?"

"I conduct horse-training clinics."

"Excellent! Doing any around here?"

"Just finished one in Missoula which made it convenient to come for this celebration."

Marv nodded. "You won't be sorry. You should stay for the book signing tomorrow at L'Amour and More. M.R. Morrison will be there, which is *so* exciting."

"I know. I get Morrison's newsletter and that's another reason I'm here. She's my favorite author."

"Well, Harry, I think we have us a winner. She admires Morrison's books and our branding. Stick around as long as you want, Jordan."

"That would be lovely, except my business keeps me on the move. I have a clinic in Bozman next week."

"Our loss, their gain," Harry said. "But just so you know, on Labor Day the town—"

"They're coming! They're coming!" A little boy in the street hopped up and down and pointed as *Stars and Stripes Forever* ended the waves of conversation. Everyone stood.

She was five-eight and she'd worn boots with two-inch heels or she would've been blocked. It helped that all the cowboys took off their hats when the two lead horses approached bearing the US and Montana flags.

Both horses behaved beautifully considering the blue and gold bedecked color guard twirling flags behind them and the band's extremely loud rendition of the Souza tune. Several members of the crowd, likely band parents, whooped and cheered as they drew closer.

Was that Adam Bridger on the roan gelding? She'd checked out the Mustang Valley website last week and that sure looked like the town's new mayor. If it was, then the redhead riding the white horse had to be his wife, Tracy. Luis had said his family was *kind of a big deal* in this town. Clearly.

If it weren't for M.R. Morrison's newsletters, she wouldn't be here. When Morrison had promoted the Hearts & Hooves digital adoption program, she'd adopted three horses.

Then came the announcement of the book signing on July fifth. Her clinic in Missoula ended on July second. Had the Universe been telling her to spend the Fourth of July weekend in Mustang Valley?

Kinda seemed like it. She'd booked the hotel beginning the night of the third and signed up for Sunday's tour of the wild horse sanctuary.

Then she'd had The Dream.

Luis had appeared looking as incredibly handsome as she remembered, his dark eyes glowing with passion. *Come to me, querida,* he'd murmured in the velvet tones that coaxed horses to behave and women to swoon. *We belong together.* Then he'd vanished.

After that night, she'd reluctantly admitted to herself he'd been in the back of her mind when she'd adopted those horses. Contributing to a cause he was involved in gave her a tingle of pleasure. She'd love to see him again.

Not to rekindle the flame, of course. He was likely married by now. He could have kids.

Spending the holiday weekend in his hometown would be the ideal venue to reconnect and find out how he was doing. He'd been a bright spot in her life. It would be great to catch up.

She'd emailed him through the H&H website so she wouldn't catch him by surprise. She'd hoped his response would give her a clue about his status. Not that it mattered, but it would have been good to know in advance.

His cheerful reply had been as informative as a blank highway marker. She'd just have to find out his personal situation the old-fashioned way, face-to-face. That was okay, too.

"Wow! Jordan, look at that!" Harry pointed toward a wagon coming into view behind a troupe of enthusiastic bagpipers.

"Whoa. Incredible!" Mounted in the back of the wagon was a 3-D, life-sized replica of H&H's running horse logo.

"Bet Xavier did it," Marv said. "That kid has the touch." He leaned toward her. "Zay's part of the Bridger Bunch. Ever hear of that crew?"

"I have, actually. I digitally adopted horses from H&H and I'm taking the tour on Sunday."

"Good for you. Great cause."

She admired the matched pair of horses pulling the wagon. "Those are gorgeous palominos."

"That's Spence Bridger's team, Woody and Buzz," Harry said. "They've been in every parade for the last fifteen years, at least. His oldest daughter Mila drives them these days."

Because Spence was gone. The mention of his name reminded her she hadn't offered her condolences to Luis during their brief email exchange. Hadn't felt right. She'd do it in person, though, assuming they'd have any private time to talk.

She recognized Claudette from pictures on the website. The crowd shouted with excitement as she threw caps like frisbees and shot bundled T-shirts out of a hand-held cannon. One sailed over everyone's head and hit Jordan in the face.

She yelped in surprise but managed to catch it before it hit the pavement.

"Bullseye!" Marv shouted, laughing.

"This is awesome." She shook it out to admire the black running horse on a white background. "A little big for me, but I don't care."

"Hey, quit looking at your T-shirt." Harry gave her a nudge. "You don't want to miss what's coming next."

The woman driving the flatbed rolling toward them looked familiar. Of course she did. She had Luis's deep-set eyes and his chiseled cheekbones.

One hand firmly controlled the matched set of bays as she waved to the crowd, her face alight with joy. Had to be his mom, Raquel.

Cheers and applause greeted the flatbed as it glided by the hotel. Jordan draped the T-shirt over her shoulder and clapped until her hands were sore. What a heartfelt tribute to the nation's female icons, especially portrayed by four women in their seventies or eighties. They must be Luis's grandma and his three aunties.

He'd talked about them with great love. The suffragette brandished her *Give Women the Vote* sign and Rosie the Riveter flexed her muscles. Then they showered bystanders with candy. Betsy Ross did her best to throw out candy but was kept busy making sure the huge flag on her lap didn't drag on the floor.

Whenever Lady Liberty tossed out a handful, her drapery slipped to reveal a star-spangled bikini. The crowd loved it and yelled for more candy. Marv put two fingers in his mouth and gave her a whistle of approval.

Jordan pegged her as Luis's Aunt Kat. The names of the others hadn't stuck, but stories about Luis's irrepressible aunt, a former runway model, had stayed with her.

As the flatbed moved on by, she read their glittering banner. *Dazzling Damsels.* What a kick. She could see why Luis was so enamored of this place and his family.

She kept her attention on the flatbed as it reached the corner and made the turn on its way around the square. But a feeling of being watched made her look to her right.

Luis. She gulped. Had he seen her? Maybe not. He gave no indication of it.

He was the same but not the same. He'd added muscle, especially in his chest and broad shoulders. The years fell away and her body warmed with the remembered sensation of that chest brushing hers.

Not the reaction she needed to be having right now! Safer to focus on his horse.

The butterscotch pinto he rode with such confidence was Scout, clearly older and wiser just like her horse Fudge. The two geldings had mixed it up during that clinic. Their riders had mixed it up in a totally different way.

Scout still had fire in him, made plain by his arched neck and tendency to prance. But the gelding was more controlled than he'd been five years ago.

The same could be said of his rider. Then Luis turned his head. His dark gaze held hers for one heart-stopping moment, sending heat pouring through her.

He still had fire in him, too. Her unruly body responded to that searing look the same way it had five years ago. If that cowboy had a wife or a girlfriend, he'd just cheated on them in his head.

He broke eye contact and faced forward, his profile achingly familiar. Since he was on her side of the street, she automatically checked his left hand. No ring.

Didn't mean anything. If he'd been part of setting up for the parade entry, he might have left it off. Rings could be a hazard when working with horses. She lectured her racing heart to settle down. They'd looked at each other. Big deal.

But as he passed by, he swiveled in the saddle, searching her out again. She waved at him because she couldn't help it. He tipped his hat.

Then he moved on, his relaxed riding style touching off more memories. Sexy cowboy. Sexy lover. He had to be married. Men like Luis were snapped up quick.

Belatedly she took note of the riders with him. The blonde woman in front must be Greta, the youngest Bridger. The other three would be Monty, Xavier and Rio. They all looked alike from the back except Luis. She'd know those buns anywhere.

Since he'd returned her wave with a tip of his hat, she might as well take the guesswork out of the situation. The sooner she knew his marital status the better.

She rolled up her T-shirt and tucked it in her backpack. "Harry, Marv, thank you so much for making room for me. I'm gonna leave you guys and head toward the staging area so I can meet someone when they get back."

Harry chuckled. "Luis Bridger, I presume?"

"Um, yes." Her cheeks warmed. "Haven't seen him in years. It'll be good to catch up."

"Judging from his reaction to seeing you, he'll be quite happy to do that." Marv's eyes sparkled. "FYI, he's still single."

"He is?" Damn, her voice had squeaked. For sure her face was bright red by now.

"He is." Marv beamed at her. "Barbers know everything about everybody. He was seeing someone last year but it didn't work out. She wasn't right for him."

And neither am I. But that knowledge did nothing to smother the fire Luis's hot glance had started. "Um, well, that's nice. For him, I mean. Not for us." She was rambling. "Because there is no us. We're only—"

"Old friends reconnecting." Harry patted her on the shoulder. "Don't mind Marv. He's a romantic. Cool it, Marv. You're embarrassing our new friend."

"Sorry, Jordan. It's just that the minute I saw that look pass between you two I got a squiggle in my tummy. You belong together. I could be wrong, of course. I never am, but there's always a first time."

What a sweet guy. "The truth is, Luis and I are on different paths." Which hadn't changed.

But he'd telegraphed interest just now. Maybe there was a chance they could pick up where they'd left off, share another short but incredible weekend together.

Marv shrugged. "Time will tell. Hope to see you around this weekend."

"I'm sure you will." With a smile and two thumbs up, she turned and threaded her way through the packed throng.

"Go to the high school parking lot!" Harry called after her.

"Thanks!" Once she made it out of the square, the journey became easier. She waved at a Girl Scout troop marching in formation and they waved back.

Groups on horseback were more common than wagons. Some riders advertised a business and others were clearly a family, often in matching outfits.

The two-story red brick high school was about a block away as she passed a wagon full of older men in Stetsons and bathing trunks.

They lounged in an empty wooden hot tub surrounded by faux icebergs made with clear plastic drop cloths. Even the wagon's driver wore only trunks and a hat. Their sign identified them as the Polar Bear Club.

The driver called to her. "You're going the wrong way, ma'am!"

"Thanks, but I'm on a mission!" she shouted back.

"Come ride with us!" yelled one of the men in the hot tub. "We've got room and we've got beer!" He lifted a can to prove it.

"That's not classy, Eli," said a chubby man sitting next to him. "I can offer you a can of excellent wine if you would care to join us?"

She walked backwards for a few paces. "No, but thanks for the offer. Enjoy the parade."

"We will!" the first man called out, saluting her with his beer.

She hurried on, all thoughts of the Polar Bear Club vanishing as she passed the final entry in the parade, a street sweeper, and walked through the open gate of the high school parking lot. Her pulse was elevated, like she'd been running rather than walking.

When Luis came back to the staging area, he'd be with the rest of his family. Would he introduce her to them? If so, how? As a fellow horse trainer he'd met at a clinic five years ago? A good friend from the past?

Only one way to find out.

She had no trouble locating two large goose-neck horse trailers hitched to trucks sporting the Laughing Creek logo. Propping her hips against the fender of the nearest LCR truck, she settled in to wait.

3

When Luis spotted Jordan in the staging areas, he instinctively pulled back on the reins. Then he took a breath and nudged Scout forward into the high school parking lot.

She stood next to his truck talking to Adam and Tracy. Seeing her riled him up something fierce.

Greta glanced over her shoulder. "Anybody know who that blonde lady is?"

"Nope," Zay and Rio said in unison.

Monty eyed him. "How about you, bro?"

He spoke just loud enough for Monty to hear. "Jordan Sterling. Met her at a clinic years ago."

"She's a friend of Luis's!" Monty called out to the others. Then he lowered his voice. "Figured you knew her. You don't usually stare at random strangers, let alone tip your hat. Did you know she was coming?"

"Yes, at least that she planned to. I didn't mention it because I figured it was no big deal."

"Tell that to someone who didn't see your reaction to spotting her. Or the way you tipped your hat. Looks like the lady took it as an invitation."

"She waved. I couldn't just ignore her."

"She waved because you turned to take another look."

He sighed. "Yeah, I did." He was so screwed. "Adam's gotta wonder what the heck's going on."

"Just play it cool. I've got your back."

"Thanks." Now Monty was aware this meeting had tied him in knots. Would his family see that? Probably. Would Jordan? Yep.

His brothers and sisters congregated around Jordan. The Dazzling Damsels, thankfully, had their own crowd of fans to keep them busy and his mom was involved with that hubbub. But sooner or later she'd notice her family gathered around a stranger and come to investigate. He needed to get ahead of that.

He glanced at Monty. "Here goes nothin'." Swinging out of the saddle and dropping the reins to the ground, he approached the knot of people. "Hey, you made it!"

Adam looked his way. "There he is. Did I miss you mentioning you had a friend coming in this weekend?"

"No. I didn't tell anyone. Sorry." And now he really wished he had. He could have avoided the curious looks he was getting from his siblings.

He avoided all of them, meeting Jordan's gaze. The warmth in her blue eyes was a sucker punch that left him breathless. Just like the first time. Nothing had changed. He wanted her more than ever. And it looked like she wanted him, too.

She was saying something. He had to force himself to concentrate on her words and not the tempting curve of her lips.

"No apology necessary. You and I both know traveling with a horse makes travel plans unpredictable. I could have been held up in Missoula if I'd had issues with Fudge."

"Is he here?" He surveyed the parking lot, as if she might have ridden him down from Missoula and left him tied to the fence while she watched the parade.

"I stabled him up in Missoula. They had a spot for my trailer, too. Easier that way."

"I wish we'd known," Claudie said. "You could have saved yourself some money and trailered him out to the ranch." Her quick glance in his direction was clear. He should've made that offer.

"That's incredibly generous, but dropping in on a person I haven't seen in five years and expecting his family to provide a place for me and my horse seems—"

"Perfectly normal to us." The chiding look Mila sent him was even sharper than Claudie's. "You could go get him right now, but I'd hate for you to miss out on the festivities."

Hey, he could redeem himself and buy some necessary breathing room in the process. Jordan was even more potent than she'd been five years ago. "Let me fetch him. Just call them and then write me a note I can give to whoever's in charge."

"Oh, no, I couldn't. My trailer's set up for a gooseneck connection and—"

"So's mine." He gestured to it. "Or I could take your truck if you wouldn't mind. Seriously, that's the answer. I couldn't go right this minute, since I need to get our horses back to the ranch. But after that I—"

"That's very sweet, but I wouldn't consider it. This is your town's celebration and you should be here to enjoy it." Her jaw firmed the way it had when she'd told him it would be better if they called it quits.

"Even more reason. You've never been here on the Fourth and I've seen every one since I was five. I can afford to miss a little of it. I'll be happy to run up there." It would give her a chance to get to know his family a bit, and he'd have time to figure out what he wanted to do about the attraction sparking between them.

"Thanks, but I can't accept. Please stay and have fun."

"Speaking of that." Adam checked the time on his phone. "Trace and I need to take off. We promised to help set up the dunking booth so it's ready by noon. We only came back here to load Banjo and Moonlight, so we'd better get to it."

"We'll take care of your horses." Zay grinned. "We don't want you to miss a second of your allotted time in that booth."

"Gee, thanks." Adam made a face. "I'm counting on you guys to pay your five bucks and waste all three pitches."

"That's the plan, big brother." Rio deadpanned his comment.

"Sure is." Mila smiled. "Right, Claudie?"

"You are so right, sis."

Greta pressed her lips together, clearly trying not to laugh.

Preoccupied by Jordan's arrival, Luis had forgotten Adam had volunteered for dunking booth duty. It was tradition for the mayor, the high school principal and the chief of their volunteer fire department to trade off time in the booth.

Their dad used to do it every year he'd served as mayor, and they'd all taken great delight in nailing him. Now it was Adam's turn.

"Okay, then, we're outta here." Adam touched the brim of his hat. "Thanks for taking care of Banjo and Moonlight."

"Better stop at the dunking booth first thing," Tracy called over her shoulder. "He'll only be there two hours."

"Two very long hours." Adam let out a sigh as they walked away holding hands.

Mila gazed after them. "They're adorable." Then she turned back to the group. "Time to gather up Mom, Grandma and the aunties."

"What for?" Clearly he was missing something else he was supposed to know about.

"Claudie, Greta and I are heading back to town for the meeting with the out-of-town H&H supporters and they all want to come. We're gathering at the Raccoon for drinks and snacks before things get rolling on the square. Jordan, you're coming, right?"

"I was planning to."

"I remember now." Luis worked like hell to focus as his peripheral vision recorded the flutter of Jordan's eyelashes, the rise and fall of her chest, the pink flush on her cheeks. "Am I supposed to be there?"

"We weren't expecting you to come, but you're welcome if you want to. It would give you and Jordan a chance to catch up."

Holy hell. He desperately needed to talk with Jordan, but not at some social event where they could only exchange pleasantries. Was he affecting her the way she was affecting him? He thought so, but lust might be causing him to imagine something that wasn't there. Then again, she'd been waiting for him in the parking lot....

"No pressure, though," Mila said.

He cleared his throat. "Sounds like fun, but I'm sure we'll find time to talk later in the day. I need to get the horses back to the ranch."

"We can handle it, *hermano*." Zay's smile said he was enjoying the heck out of his brother's obvious infatuation. "Just give Monty the keys to your truck and we'll haul these critters home, no problem."

"It'll go faster with all four of us." He drilled Zay with a look.

"He's right," Monty said. "The sooner we take care of them, the sooner we'll be back to dunk our big brother."

"Good point." Claudie gathered her hair into a ponytail and pulled it through the back of her H&H cap. "Let's leave these guys to it. C'mon, Jordan. Time for you to meet our very own Dazzling Damsels."

"I can't wait."

As they headed for the flatbed, he caught himself watching Jordan walk away. Which is why he saw her quick peek at him over her shoulder.

It lit him up like a sparkler.

Turning, he faced three knowing smiles. "It's not like that."

Their smiles widened.

"It's not, dammit. We're old news." He tugged his hat lower. "*Andale.* These critters won't load themselves."

Grinning, they split up and got started. Moments later their mom beeped the horn as she drove by in the ranch van. Happy chatter spilled out the open windows. He had no trouble picking out Jordan's voice, or her laughter, which arrowed straight to his groin. If he didn't get some distance and control, he was going to embarrass himself.

The prospect of sending Adam plunging into the dunking booth motivated his brothers to move quickly. In short order they'd loaded the horses, rolled the wagon onto the flatbed and tied it down.

Zay's F-350 was hitched to the other horse trailer. Rio was driving their dad's old truck, towing the flatbed and wagon.

Monty hopped in with Luis. No surprise there. His brother would be full of questions.

That was fine. It would be a relief to talk this out instead of dealing with the ping-pong match going on in his head.

Monty stayed quiet as Luis carefully drove his rig through the parking lot gate and made his way down crowded streets to the road that led out of town. Zay followed and Rio brought up the rear, each taking it slow.

Once their caravan reached the smooth two-lane headed for Laughing Creek, Monty sighed. "It was a good parade."

"It was." Tension slowly drained away and he took a deep breath. "Maybe the best ever." He glanced over at Monty, who gave a nod.

His brother had laid his hat on the dash, leaving a noticeable sweaty crease in his light brown hair, just like their dad used to get. He could see their dad in Monty and Adam, and a little bit in Claudie and Greta.

He didn't get that crease, at least not that anyone would notice. Neither did Zay or Rio or Mila. They'd all inherited their mom's hair—dark, thick and curly.

"I'm gonna assume you two got friendly during that clinic."

His gut tightened a little. "We did. But there was no future in it. She's traveling around giving clinics, which requires being constantly on the road. I checked her website. She's deep into that."

"So still no future?"

"Right."

"Is this a booty call?"

"I... don't know. Maybe."

"You okay with that?"

"Still deciding."

"Well, she's gorgeous and she's here. Seems like if you tell yourself from the get-go that it's temporary, you could have some fun. She certainly was into you."

A wave of heat brought back the tension he'd sloughed off. "Even if she is, I'm not sure of the logistics. This is a family-focused weekend."

"During the day. But at night? You have your own house. She likely has a hotel room. Not exactly a big hurdle."

He had a good point.

"For what it's worth, if she's willing, I think you'd be crazy to pass up the opportunity."

He let out a breath. "Just have some fun, huh?"

Monty shrugged. "Why not? You've been working really hard and right now you have a rare break and some free time. Why not take advantage of the opportunity?"

4

Heading off to the Raccoon with the Bridger matriarchs and Luis's sisters without having a private moment to talk to Luis first hadn't been Jordan's plan. However, it might work out well. She could learn a lot about Luis's current situation from his family.

While she chatted with everyone about the parade and the festivities yet to come, she processed her recent encounter with the man who could arouse her with a single glance. Still.

Clearly he was affected by her, too. But he hadn't said a word to his family about her, which indicated he wasn't certain where they stood. Neither was she, exactly. He also didn't seem any more prepared than she was to handle the heat they generated.

At twenty-three she'd welcomed their spontaneous affair, a three-day adventure with no backstory and no future. Well, they had a backstory now. Her arrival in town had put a fine point on that.

They needed a private discussion so she could find out if they were still on the same page.

Taking a deep breath, she filed into the Raccoon with the Bridger women and the handful of out-of-town supporters, mostly women.

The staff had pushed several tables together and laid out munchies. Mila took one end, Claudette and Raquel took the other and Jordan opted for a spot midway down the table.

"Is this seat taken?" Luis's Aunt Kat, or Kat as she'd introduced herself when they'd met, appeared to her left, still in costume but minus her torch.

"Sure isn't. I'd love to have you sit there."

"Thank you." She slid gracefully onto the wooden chair and adjusted her drape. "This outfit is more comfortable and practical than I expected."

"It's gorgeous."

"She just wore it to drive Eli crazy." Ezzie took the seat on her other side.

She'd heard that name before. "Is he a member of the Polar Bear Club?"

"He's the head of it."

Kat let out a gusty sigh. "To think I campaigned to become a member of that motley crew. Their entry was a rolling nightmare. Curdled my eyeballs. Those old boys wouldn't know class if it bit 'em on the tuchus."

"Well, they made me laugh." Luis's Grandma Doris took the seat across from Kat. "Pretending to be drunk on non-alcoholic beer and wine."

"Was it non-alcoholic?" Carmen joined them, grabbing the vacant seat beside Doris. "I couldn't tell."

"Oh, yeah." Doris adjusted her ruffled cap. "Betty wasn't gonna let 'em have the real thing. Not on her watch." She leaned toward Jordan. "Betty's on the town council and she's been the parade marshal since God was a child."

"She clearly knows her stuff. I loved that parade." What a kick to be surrounded by the Dazzling Damsels.

As the waitstaff circulated taking drink orders and the discussion of the parade continued, her anxiety about Luis faded into the background. She sipped her coffee and enjoyed a brownie.

Putting down her coffee mug, Kat shifted in her seat. "Jordan, I've been dying to ask you something. It's extremely nosy, so you can tell me to mind my own business and I won't be offended."

Hello, anxiety. Welcome back. "Well, I—"

"Jordan's likely too polite to say that so I will." Doris gave Kat a look. "Mind your own business."

"But we're all wondering why our sweet, considerate Luis failed to mention that he knew this lovely young woman or that she was coming for the weekend."

"That's between Jordan and *mi sobrino,*" Carmen said. "They can tell us if they want. Or not."

"Exactly." Ezzie leaned around Jordan to get Kat's attention. "Let it go. Jordan doesn't—"

"Hey, it's okay." She'd started this ball rolling, so she might as well take the mystery out of the situation. These ladies could inform his mom and sisters later when they weren't busy talking with the other H&H supporters.

She cleared her throat. "Luis and I had… a very special time during a horse-training clinic five years ago, and—"

"Ahhh, I knew it." Kat smiled. "I knew it. You—"

"Let her finish." Doris gave her a look.

"We were headed in different directions and didn't plan to see each other again. When I popped up on his radar, he probably didn't know what it meant or what to do."

Kat's eyes sparkled with eagerness "What does it mean? Are you—"

"Kat!" Doris glared at her.

"Luis and I are still headed in different directions. I have a thriving business that keeps me on the road. We're… friends. I didn't come here for him. I came for the celebration, the M.R. Morrison signing and the H&H tour." Mostly. Sort of.

Kat let out a disappointed sigh.

"We haven't talked in five years. For all I knew he was with someone, maybe even married."

"He should be," Ezzie said. "He's just picky."

Kat eyed Jordan. "Or he's carrying a torch for a certain—" She gave a jolt, like Doris might have kicked her under the table, dislodging her crown. She made a grab for it. "Speaking of carrying torches, my arm's sore."

"I'll be Lady Liberty next year, Kat." Ezzie leaned around Jordan. "My arm's in great shape. I can handle that torch, no *problemo*."

"But the Statue of Liberty has to be tall. You're not tall."

"Of course the statue has to be tall," Carmen sized up her sister. "That's so ships can see the glow of her torch and not run into that island she stands on. Who knows if she was tall in real life?"

"She was modeled after a goddess." Doris put her ruffled cap in her lap.

"And how tall are they supposed to be?" Ezzie peered across the table at Doris.

She shrugged. "No idea. Never met one."

"Other than me." Kat adjusted her crown again. "I've been told by several men that I'm—"

"Are you immortal?" Ezzie lifted her eyebrows.

"In some circles."

"Not in this one," Doris said.

"So nobody's seen an actual goddess." Ezzie flashed a triumphant smile. "There could be a goddess who's short like me or medium-sized like Carmen. I can be Lady Liberty. I'll just cut off some of that silver drape and—"

"Hello, everyone," Mila called out from her end of the table. "And welcome."

Ezzie moved closer to Jordan. "See what I did there?" she whispered as Mila continued with her opening remarks.

"No," Jordan murmured back.

"Kept the talk going and saved you from Kat, *amiga*. Watch out for her. She's a matchmaker."

"Picked up on that." She sent Ezzie a smile before giving her attention to Mila.

"I'm excited to have you all here," Mila said. "Now that we all have beverages and snacks, I'll introduce my family and then I'd like each of you to introduce yourselves."

When Jordan's turn came, she gave M.R. Morrison credit for alerting her to H&H and didn't mention her connection to Luis. Three of the other five women also had heard about the sanctuary through Morrison's newsletter.

"Okay, Claudie." Mila glanced down to the other end of the table. "Tell everyone how you came up with this adoption plan."

"It was thanks to M.R. Morrison. She put a piece in her newsletter about the Sheldrick Wildlife Trust in Kenya and its adoption program for orphaned elephants. I decided we could do the same thing with wild horses."

"Brilliant, right?" Mila said. "Except those elephant babies live in a contained area, convenient for naming and photos. Our wild horses are scattered all over the place and tend to be camera shy."

"Yeah." Claudette laughed. "I'm sure there were times Mila and Luis wished I'd kept that brilliant idea to myself. We spent months taking pictures and naming horses."

"So worth it, though," said a trim, white-haired woman. "I've sent donations here before, but it didn't feel very personal. Adopting a horse, or in my case five, makes it so real."

"It *is* real." Mila sat forward, her expression eager. "On Sunday you'll see for yourselves."

"I can't *wait*," said a thirty-something woman who dressed in bright colors. "You two are amazing. Let's all give them a big hand!"

After the applause died down, Claudette opened a large tote and passed out caps and T-shirts to anyone who wanted them. Jordan asked for a cap. Then she pulled her T-shirt from her backpack and described getting nailed by the cannon, which made Claudette laugh.

Before the group broke up, the visitors each grabbed a moment to change in the bathroom so everyone except the Dazzling Damsels left wearing H&H T-shirts and caps. Jordan enjoyed the heck out of their display of camaraderie. Bonding over a love of animals was pretty cool.

On the way out, Kat was right behind her. "Jordan, can I have a minute?"

"Of course." She stepped to one side of the door.

Kat looked her in the eye. They were almost exactly the same height. "I'll bet Ezzie warned you that I'd try to play matchmaker this weekend."

"She did."

"Well, I won't."

"Oh?"

"Marriage was never for me, but when I see two people who are obviously perfect for each other, I can't resist playing Cupid. That said, I respect your ambition and dedication to making it on your own."

"Thank you."

"You remind me of me. Single-minded, in every sense of the word. I wouldn't dream of interfering."

"I appreciate that."

"I'm also crazy about Luis." Kat's eyes gleamed with fierce, protective love.

"I promise to be very, very careful."

"Good." She linked her arm through Jordan's. "Let's check out the dunking booth. I've been working on my fastball."

5

Returning to town after the parade had always been the highlight of the day for Luis. No more performance anxiety. Nothing to do but have fun.

There would be a country band playing in the gazebo and mouthwatering food for sale. Booths offered all the games he loved and was good at.

When he was a kid he'd kept the prizes for himself. When he got older he'd given them away, mostly to girls.

Surrounded by a posse of family and friends, cash stuffed in his pockets, he'd always joined the noisy crowd with eager anticipation.

This time, he had Monty's comments rolling around in his head, adding a new layer of anticipation to the festivities.

He wanted to clarify the situation with Jordan, ASAP. He wouldn't be able to relax and enjoy the rest of the day until he knew where he stood.

They'd been gone almost two hours, though, so the dunking booth had to come first. It was easy to spot because it had the longest line and biggest crowd of onlookers. He and his brothers headed in that direction.

Off to his left he spotted a group of women wearing H&H T-shirts and caps. His chest tightened. Jordan would be in that group. He forced himself to look away, not wanting to spot her. Not yet.

Monty located the end of the line and they chose to go youngest to oldest — Rio first and Luis last. As he took his place behind Zay and gazed at Adam perched in the dunking booth, the idea of getting dunked in cold water sounded like a good one. It might be the only way to cool his jets regarding Jordan.

Besides, the sun was hot today. It would feel good. Adam also had Tracy there handing out the softballs and keeping him company.

Adam had switched to bathing trunks and an old straw hat of their dad's that was now completely waterlogged. Laughing and cracking jokes, he looked happy, just like their dad had been when he'd done it.

Monty sucked in a breath. "Damn. If you squint a little, that could be Dad up there."

"Yeah." Zay sounded subdued. "I guess it's the hat. I didn't know it was still around."

"It's not just the hat," Rio said. "It's his laugh, the way he tilts his head. I don't know if I can dunk him."

"You gotta, little brother." Monty squeezed his shoulder. "We're doing this just like we used to."

"Okay. You're right."

"What if we do it blindfolded?" Luis glanced at his brothers. "Remember? We tried that one year."

"And you were the only one who hit the target, Mr. All-State Pitcher." Zay shook his head. "No blindfold for me, but you go right ahead."

"Believe I will." It would add an element of challenge to the event and provide a distraction until he could talk to Jordan.

The line moved fast because the folks ahead of them all had lousy aim. Adam began to dry off. Then Rio stepped up.

Adam grinned. "Remember what we talked about, little brother."

"Nice hat, Adam. Too bad it's gonna get wet." Rio sounded like his old self, but his first throw went wide.

"Excellent!" Adam called out. "Two more, just like that!"

"You wish!" Rio hit the target dead center and Adam tumbled into the water.

Monty and Zay only needed one throw each. Adam's hat was so soggy the brim almost covered his face.

"Hey, there, Luis." Adam took off the hat and squeezed out some of the water. "Take it easy on me, okay?"

That brought a lump to his throat. Consciously or unconsciously, Adam had repeated the words their dad used to say every year because he had the best arm in the family.

"Which is why I'm giving myself a handicap, *hermano*." While studying the position of the target, he pulled a blue bandana from his hip pocket, folded it and tied it behind his head.

"Way to even the odds, Luis!" called someone from the crowd of onlookers.

Belatedly he realized his bandana stunt would draw attention. Not his goal. Too late, now. He palmed the softball Tracy handed him.

Although it was larger than the baseball he'd spent years hurling across the plate, that didn't affect his method. He'd nurtured his ability to visualize the throw in advance. Then he let instinct take over.

The moment the ball left his hand, he knew exactly where it was going. He didn't have to hear Adam's yell or the splash to know he'd hit the target. He also got a round of applause.

Taking off the blindfold, he tucked it in his pocket, stepped out of line and joined his brothers. "Guess it wasn't much of a handicap, after all."

"Yeah, we know." Monty smiled. "You just can't help being cool."

"Luis?"

He glanced in the direction of a voice he recognized all too well. His eager heart thumped faster. "Hey, Jordan."

She made her way through the crowd toward him. Her white T-shirt with the running horse logo ballooned out from her slim body but she'd worn it anyway. Endearing. The white H&H cap looked adorable, too.

Her enthusiastic adoption of his family's cause added another layer of attraction. Obviously he wouldn't have to go looking for her, though. He greeted her with a smile. "How are you liking the celebration so far?"

Her answering smile encompassed him and his brothers. "It's great. That was a neat trick with the blindfold."

"You saw that?"

"He's the best pitcher Mustang Valley's ever seen, or ever will, most likely." Rio puffed out his chest. "He took the Mustangs to the state championship two years in a row."

"Really?" She gave him an assessing look. "That's the first I've heard of it."

"Because my brother doesn't brag, so I have to do it for him. I'm Rio. You must be Jordan."

"Guilty as charged."

"That's Monty." Rio pointed. "And Zay. Monty's the vet for H&H and Zay created that awesome horse float for the parade."

Jordan nodded. "That was incredible. I've heard several folks talking about that horse."

"That's nice to hear." Zay blushed.

"They're speculating on how you can possibly top that."

"I already told him how." Rio stuck his hands in his pockets and tilted back on his bootheels. "*Two* running horses."

"That would be breathtaking."

"We'll see."

She'd completely charmed his brothers. And him. He needed to get her alone before he totally lost perspective. "I don't know about anyone else, but I'm ready for something to drink. Plus I owe Jordan one."

"By all means get something to drink," Monty said. "While you're gone, the rest of us can look awesome knocking over milk bottles and busting balloons."

"Ain't that the truth." Zay chuckled. "Every year I think I'm gonna show up my big brother and every year I get my ass whipped."

He smiled. "Maybe this is the year."

"Not after that blindfold trick. Jordan, do us a favor and get this cowboy out of here."

"Be glad to. Now that I think about it, I'm really thirsty."

"Then let's do something about that." He tipped his hat to his brothers. "See you guys later."

She fell into step beside him and tossed a *nice to meet you* over her shoulder.

"Nice meeting you, too!" Rio called out as they walked away.

Jordan lowered her voice. "Do you really want something to drink or was that an excuse?"

"Both. How about you?"

"Same."

"Alcohol or non?"

"Non. I want to keep my wits about me."

"Gotcha. Lemonade?"

"Perfect."

"The stand's right over there." He pointed to it. "Did you have fun at the meeting this morning?"

"I had a blast. Your grandma and aunties are something else."

"I knew you'd get along with them." Her scent, light and flowery, stirred memories that had him thinking inappropriate thoughts for the public setting. "I'm sorry I didn't mention you to anybody—"

"Kat thinks it's because you're still carrying a torch."

"She does?" He hadn't considered his reaction in those terms. Or that his aunties would have already formed an opinion about it.

"Ezzie warned me that Kat's a matchmaker."

"That's a fact. I'll have a talk with her. I don't want her—"

"You don't have to."

"I think I do."

"She promised not to interfere after I explained our situation."

"No kidding?" He stopped in his tracks. "What did you say?"

"That we recognized five years ago that a relationship wouldn't work. We have different goals. I'm here for the holiday celebration, the H&H tour and the M.R. Morrison signing. Period."

That set him back. "So I have nothing to do with your decision to drive down here?"

A soft blush made her eyes look very blue. "I wouldn't say *nothing*. I like you. I was curious about how things were going for you. And ever since I learned about your dad, I've wanted to—"

"When did you find out?"

"When I went on the site to adopt the horses. There's that beautiful page dedicated to him." Her gaze softened. "I'm so sorry, Luis. I could tell you idolized him."

"I did." Her empathy touched a very tender place in his heart. He cleared his throat. "I still do.

Whenever I'm working with the horses, I hear his voice."

"That's lovely."

He damned near pulled her into his arms. He'd forgotten how easily he dropped his guard when she looked at him like that, as if he was the only person in the world.

Within minutes of being alone with her, he'd lost himself in the soothing warmth of her gaze. He felt validated, understood. *Seen.*

At twenty-five he'd thought his obsession with her was based on sex appeal. But he was beginning to suspect Jordan aroused a response that went much deeper. He had no strategy for controlling it, and if he didn't find one soon, no telling what kind of fool he might make of himself.

Forcing himself to break eye contact, he tugged down the brim of his hat. "We should get that lemonade."

6

"Yes, we should." Jordan was very curious what Luis was thinking, but she didn't ask. Instead, she accepted the large glass of lemonade he bought her and suggested they go find a shady spot where they could sit and talk. Holding the lemonade in both hands would help her keep her mitts off him.

Wouldn't be easy. With every passing minute, she felt more comfortable with him. The same thing had happened five years ago. They'd bonded quickly and the shift to an intimate relationship had been effortless, natural, and oh, so thrilling.

The square was packed, so they crossed the street and sat on the top step of the courthouse. By this time in the afternoon that much was shaded, but the cement was still warm under her tush. She set her backpack down next to her.

"This is better." Luis chose a spot an arm's length away and sat at an angle so he was almost facing her. "I like the music but it's hard to hear when you're right by it." He took a long swallow of his lemonade.

She scooted around, too, and the toes of their boots almost touched. His had some intricate stitching. Looked pricey. "Nice boots." She sipped her drink.

"Wore the fancy ones today." He glanced at hers. "Looks like you did, too. I like that color."

"They call it Montana Sky. I don't have much reason to wear them, but I've always wanted boots with fringe." She wiggled her foot to make the fringe sway.

"Bet they look great on the dance floor."

She met his gaze. A tingling started low in her stomach. "They were supposed to be, but...."

"Too slippery?"

"No, they're fine." During the clinic they'd talked about checking out the band at the local watering hole. But that would've cut into their lovemaking time and they'd nixed the idea. Those thoughts made her temperature rise. She took a big gulp of her drink. "This lemonade's tasty. Hits the spot. Thank you." She swirled the ice around to redistribute it.

"You've never taken those boots dancing, have you?"

Was he about to invite her out? "It's tough to find time in the schedule, but if you're suggesting—"

"I might be. I also have two brothers who would love to take you and those boots for a spin around the floor of the Raccoon tonight. It would be a shame to waste a perfect opportunity." Breaking eye contact, he concentrated on his drink.

"Only two brothers?" She smiled. "Who has a girlfriend?"

"Rio. That boy's been breaking hearts since he was in first grade. I'm offering Zay and Monty."

"You might want to check with them first."

"Don't need to. I can tell they like you. Everybody likes you." A soft glow lit his dark eyes. "I'll admit the prospect of your visit knocked me sideways, but I'm glad you came."

Her breath caught. Not the words he'd spoken in her dream, but the velvet tone was there, giving her all the feels. "Me, too."

He thumbed back his hat. "I never told my family about our...." He frowned. "See, that's part of the problem. I don't know how to describe—"

"Me, either. All the words are wrong."

His gaze sought hers. "They sound shallow. But it wasn't."

"Because we're not."

"Exactly! If I'd told my sisters I'd met you years ago, it wouldn't have ended there. They would've wanted details and... I have no poker face."

"I get it. I held back, too. I could have told Mila we'd met at a clinic when she emailed me to confirm my tour reservation, but I didn't. For one thing, I thought there was a good chance you'd be married with a couple of kids."

He chuckled. "I expected that, too."

"What happened? You're a great catch. I can't believe some woman hasn't—"

"Auntie Ezzie thinks I'm too picky."

"I know. She told me."

"I'll bet she did." He grinned, showing off those sexy dimples. "She accuses Auntie Kat of being a matchmaker but she's just as bad. She's been after me to find someone, especially now that Adam's married."

"Please promise me you won't end up marrying someone to please your aunties."

"I won't. I can't. It's gotta feel right. And so far...." He shrugged. "I guess I am picky."

"She'll show up. I'm glad you're waiting for someone special. You deserve that." Saying it made her chest hurt, but she ignored it.

Emotion flickered in his eyes. "Your clinic's going gangbusters. I checked out your website."

"Everything's worked out exactly as I'd hoped." She drained the last of her lemonade.

"That's good to hear. I didn't expect you to be married with kids, but...." He paused and looked away. "Never mind. None of my business." He finished off his drink, too.

"Hey, I put myself right in the middle of your business. If you're wondering if I've found anyone special, there was a guy."

"Was?"

"He was personable, fun to be with. Although I never plan to get married, I thought—"

"Wait. You don't want to get married? Ever?"

"I don't have the personality for it."

"I don't know what that means."

"It means I'm a load. I expect too much from people."

"I sure didn't see that when we were at the clinic."

"Of course not. It was only three days. Anyway I warned this guy that I expected a lot and he wasn't worried. He offered to be my front man, book the venues and help me grow my business so

I could concentrate on the thing I love best, working with horses."

"Sounds like a good arrangement."

"I thought so, but he spent money on advertising that didn't work and created a new website I hated. Then he got in a kerfuffle with the owner of one of my regular venues and I almost lost that space. We parted ways and sure enough, he said I expected too much of him."

"Sounds to me like he was inept."

"Or my expectations are too high. Bottom line, I function better when I go solo."

He gazed at her. "Not me."

"Makes sense. You grew up with the Bridger Bunch. I've been pretty much on my own my whole life."

His eyes widened. "You have? I thought you had a family."

"Strictly speaking, I did. Still do." She shifted her attention to the crowded square. Even in that mass of people, she easily located the cluster of women wearing H&H T-shirts and caps. Gave her a cozy feeling. "Nothing like yours, though."

"I figured that since you never talked about your parents. You mentioned your big brother, Cole, but his name is all I remember."

She turned back to Luis. "He's a sweetie. Works construction. Tried to talk me into training as a carpenter so we could go into business together. But carpentry isn't my jam."

"Clearly. You're a natural with horses."

"So are you. I have a vivid memory of you interacting with Scout before the clinic had started, before we'd met. You were giving him your undivided attention, connecting with him on a level I rarely see. I couldn't wait to meet you."

"My attention wasn't all that undivided. I was fascinated with how you communicated with Fudge. I knew I'd found a kindred spirit."

"Kindred spirits! What a great description. It sounds like we're connected but in a disembodied way." She looked at him. "What do you think? Can we go with that?"

He hesitated. "Do you want the truth?"

"Always."

"You're a beautiful, sexy woman and there's no way in hell I'll ever imagine you as a disembodied spirit, kindred or otherwise."

"Oh." She lapped up every syllable and was thirsty for more. "What are we going to do about it?"

"I have a few ideas. But for starters—"

Her phone chimed, making her rapidly beating heart thump even faster. "I have to take that."

"Sure."

She opened her backpack and dug out her phone. She'd silenced all calls today except from Cole or the stable and it wasn't Cole's ring. The stable wouldn't call if everything was fine. Something was wrong with Fudge.

7

Luis put down his cup. Jordan's face had lost color when her phone rang.

She huddled over her phone, listening intently to whoever was on the other line. "Just keep him quiet and I'll be there in an hour, maybe a little longer depending on traffic. Yep, thanks, Jeb. See you soon." She ended the call and tucked her phone in her backpack.

"Fudge?" He picked up his empty drink cup and stood.

"Yep." She got to her feet, hoisted her small backpack over one shoulder and grabbed her cup, too. "He's favoring his right foreleg. Jeb thinks it's a hoof abscess. Not that it's life-threatening, but I need to go up there."

"Does this guy have a vet available?"

"He's calling around to see if he can find someone. Wouldn't you know it's a holiday."

"Let us help."

"Us?"

"The Bridger Bunch. You and I can go get him and I'll alert Monty to meet us at the ranch. All his equipment and supplies are out there."

"I'm grateful for the offer, but Missoula's pretty big. We'll find someone. I won't ask Monty to give up his—"

"He'll want to. I know you like handling things yourself, but he'll want to handle this for you and Fudge."

She started down the steps. "It doesn't feel right, Luis. Hauling Fudge out to the ranch and imposing on Monty — that's not my style."

"Maybe not, but it's Monty's style." He followed her down to the sidewalk and tossed his cup in the recycling bin. "He loves riding to the rescue. Besides, Mila and Claudie will be crushed if you take off because you didn't want to bother anybody."

She put her drink cup in the bin and turned back to him, her expression skeptical. "Did you just say *crushed*?"

"Damned, straight. You're part of the H&H gang, now. You're wearing the T-shirt and the cap to prove it. You have friends here who care about you, whether you like it or not."

"I do like it, but I don't want to inconvenience—"

"Jordan." Frustration pushed him to take her by the shoulders. "If you handle this on your own, it'll be a slap in the face to everyone who would have wanted to help, including me."

Those stormy blue eyes told him a battle was going on. She took a shaky breath. "Okay. If you say so. You know them better than I do."

"Yes, ma'am, I do." He let go of her, but not before the warmth of her skin imprinted on his hands. "Better contact the stable." While he waited for her to accomplish that, he took a deep breath, hoping to rid himself of the buzzy sensation left over from touching her.

She finished her call. "Jeb was relieved that I have a vet down here. He was getting nowhere."

"I can believe it. Let's go get your truck. I'll text Monty once we're on our way."

"You're going up there with me?"

"Somebody needs to."

"No, they don't."

"It's a Bridger Bunch rule of thumb. If you're dealing with a crisis that requires you to drive somewhere, taking someone along makes sense. You could have a flat. Or a fender-bender. Even if there's no hiccup, you'll have someone to talk to so you won't worry as much."

"I'll be *fine.*"

"Want me to tap somebody else to go instead?"

"No! Honest to God, Luis, I don't need anyone to—"

"Humor me. Please."

She heaved a sigh. "Okay. I'm in the lot behind the Golden Nugget." She headed in that direction. "I don't remember you being so bossy."

"I don't remember you being so stubborn." That wasn't exactly true. He'd tried to find a way around her decision to cut off communication the day they'd said goodbye. What would've been so wrong about exchanging phone numbers?

But she'd been adamant. She hadn't wanted anything distracting her from launching her career. He'd never met someone so determined to go it alone.

Her instincts regarding him had been on target, though. If he'd had her number, he would have texted. If she'd scheduled a clinic within a hundred miles, he would've made the drive. He'd been nuts about her. Still was, obviously.

Touching her just now had fired him up. Going with her to Missoula would fan that flame.

Maybe he'd end up getting burned, but there was no reality in which he'd send her off by herself. Logic was on his side. It was a holiday. Drivers got stupid on holidays.

Jordan beeped open the lock on her shiny silver F-350, tossed her small backpack behind the seat and hopped in. He climbed in on the passenger side.

A Kenny Chesney tune poured from the dashboard speakers. She hit a switch to end the music.

"Nice rig. Good branding." *Jordan Sterling, Quality Equine Training* was lettered on each door panel.

"Thanks." She backed out slowly, checking her mirrors. She might be upset, but obviously that didn't make her careless when navigating a parking lot.

He respected that. He also respected her self-sufficiency. But it looked like she'd turned it into a religion. Why? What had happened to her?

His imagination started playing with the possibilities. Just like horses, people had reasons for their behavior. He had a hunch—

"Have you texted Monty?"

"Uh, no. No, I haven't. Doing it right now. Think I'll call instead. He might miss a text." He'd been so focused on her he'd almost blown his part of the deal.

Monty answered on the second ring. "Hey, bro—" The rest was drowned out by a mixture of country music and the boisterous crowd.

"Can you go someplace quieter? I can't hear you."

"Sure thing. Hang on." The crunch, crunch of his booted feet indicated he was on the move. A few seconds later the background noise had faded considerably. "How's that?"

"Better."

"Where are you? We looked around and you weren't on the courthouse steps anymore."

"Jordan and I are driving up to Missoula to get her horse. The guy at the stable up there thinks he's got a hoof abscess."

"Uh-oh. I assume you'll be taking him out to the ranch?"

"That's the plan. It'll be at least a couple of hours. I'll call you when we're a half-hour out."

"Perfect. See if you can get a picture of his hoof and text it to me. That'll be helpful."

"Will do."

"Great. I'll meet you out there."

"Wait. I just realized you rode in with me. I should've found you and given you the keys."

"No worries. I'll just borrow Adam's truck or Mom's van. We'll work it out. You just get that critter to the ranch. I'll take it from there."

"Thanks, *hermano.* I owe you one."

"Buy me a drink tonight and we're square. See you soon."

"You bet. 'Bye." He disconnected. "We're all set."

"You didn't even have to ask him." Her voice carried a trace of disbelief.

"When Monty finds out a horse is in trouble, there's no asking required. Unless he's incapacitated for some reason, he's on it."

"That's admirable."

"He wants me to text him a picture of his hoof if I can manage it."

"I'm sure we can. He's a sweetheart." She cleared her throat. "Listen, I apologize for my attitude just now. You were only trying to help and I gave you a hard time about it. I'm sorry."

"It's natural. You're worried about Fudge."

"I am, but that's no excuse." She sighed. "It's just that I like your family so much and I... I don't want to be a nuisance."

"You couldn't predict that Fudge would have a problem. Abscesses come out of the blue."

"Yeah, he's never had one before, but still. Please tell me Monty will let me pay him."

"Uh... well, the thing is you support H&H, so—"

"Adopting three horses is a drop in the bucket compared to what a vet would charge for treating my horse."

"Yeah, but that adoption's not a one and done type thing. We aim to keep you for years. If those horses find forever homes, we'll suggest other ones in need." Until now he hadn't thought of it that way, but unless she bailed on the adoption thing, which wasn't likely, her contact info would be perpetually on file.

Would that include her phone number? It might. And using it for personal reasons violated H&H's code of ethics. And his.

"So you're saying Monty won't accept payment?"

"That's what I'm saying. I'm buying him a beer tonight so you can buy him the second one."

"I'll do that, but I'll come up with something else."

"A sincere thank you is plenty. You don't want to insult him."

"This is difficult territory for me."

"I can see that."

"I wasn't raised like you were. I was taught to depend on myself and not expect others to carry my load."

"Nothing wrong with that."

"But you made it sound like your family would be upset if I didn't accept their help."

"It's not like they'd be mad at you." Jordan reminded him of sanctuary horses who hadn't been born wild. Instead they'd been turned loose after years of abuse. Consequently they viewed acts of kindness as a potential trap.

"You said Mila and Claudie would be crushed."

"Maybe I overstated it, but they'd be disappointed. By now they think of you as a friend and hope you feel the same about them."

"I do. They're great. Everyone is. That's why I don't want to wear out my welcome by handing them my problems."

"Friends help friends. It's the nature of the beast."

"Well, sure, but this episode with Fudge is way more than that. If he's at the ranch, then I need to be there to help care for him. My trailer has living quarters, but I can see your mom insisting I eat with—"

"She'll invite you to bunk in the house. There's plenty of room."

She groaned. "And she'll be disappointed if I stay in my trailer?"

"Quite likely."

"This is what I'm talking about. There should be an equal give and take, but everything's out of balance."

He could tell her that nobody cared except her, but she wouldn't believe him. Somebody, and he guessed it was her parents, had convinced her that everyone kept score.

Unlearning that wouldn't be easy. Maybe she wouldn't care to. But spending time with his family would show her a different perspective.

And his weekend had just gotten a lot more complicated. She'd be sleeping only steps away. As for him, he wouldn't be sleeping much at all.

_8_

"Do you have a room in the main house?" When Luis chuckled, Jordan rushed to clarify. "I wasn't asking because—"

"Are you sure about that?"

"Yes! I was only— I mean, it's logical that you—"

"I have my own place. I won't be sleeping down the hall from you."

"That's a good thing."

"All things considered, yes, it is."

She gripped the steering wheel and focused on the road ahead. Traffic was light, thank goodness. "To be clear, are we agreeing we are or are not going there?"

Silence.

Her heart rate picked up. "Luis?"

He took a deep breath and let it out. "It could be... complicated."

"Very complicated. We're not attending a clinic where we'll never see those people again. We'd be in the bosom of your family, so to speak."

"Interesting choice of words."

"Hey." She tightened her grip on the wheel. "Freudian slip?"

He was flirting with her and she liked it way too much. "Do you want to get horizontal this weekend?"

"Plenty of other options to explore, too."

"Luis!"

"Of course I want to. So do you. Is it a bad idea? Maybe. But maybe it's inevitable."

"It is *not* inevitable." Her body disagreed.

"Looks like it to me. I kept my family in the dark, but now everyone knows we've been lovers. And here we are on a road trip."

"Your choice. In fact, you were pushy."

"And I don't regret it. I'm also glad you'll be staying at the ranch. You'll love it out there. Before your room in town kept you out of reach."

"I still am. I'll be at your mom's house and you'll be in your place."

"That's... true."

He said it like that wasn't the barrier she imagined. She couldn't help being curious about this house of his. "What's your place like?"

"It's a casita. There's a walled patio in front, a beehive fireplace in the living room, arched doorways, Mexican tile. My dad was the builder but we all helped. Most everything at Laughing Creek is a family project."

"That's why I expected there would be one big rambling house and everybody lived there." With that setup she would've had safety in numbers, even if he happened to be right down the hall. Instead he had his own, very private dwelling.

"We were all crammed in together when Mom and Dad first got married — six kids and Grandma Doris, who was a big help the first couple of years. Then six became eight when Rio and Greta came along and Dad built Grandma Doris her own cottage."

"Were the aunties part of all that?"

"They showed up later. Dad built each of them a house, too. After he died, the four of them got this idea that Dad's adult kids might like to live in those houses and each have our own place. They talked us into it by reminding us we'd helped construct three of them."

"Who lived in the one you have?"

"Auntie Carmen. Zay got Auntie Ezzie's, Monty got Grandma Doris's and Rio got Auntie Kat's."

"And they all moved into the ranch house?"

"No, they wanted the bunkhouse. They fixed it up and named it the Dorm for Dazzling Damsels. That's when they came up with their official brand."

"But if only four of you got houses, that's not very—" She stopped herself from saying *fair.* "Sorry, that's none of my business."

"No worries. Mila and Claudie already had a place. Mila inherited the mini-hacienda Dad built for my Grandma Paloma and invited Claudie to move in with her."

"Your dad sounds like a wannabe contractor. That's a lot of houses."

"There was one more. He lured his Grandma Lucy to the ranch with a modern version of the log cabin she grew up in. She was in her nineties and had health issues but resisted leaving her beloved Victorian."

"Let me guess. That's where the bookstore is."

"Yes, ma'am. It stood empty for years until Adam came up with this idea. Grandma Lucy would have approved. Dad would have, too."

"I took a walk out there last night. It's stunning. Who inherited Grandma Lucy's log cabin?"

"Adam. That's where he and Tracy live."

"Then everyone's accounted for except Greta."

"She's happy at the ranch house keeping Mom company. She's always loved the big house, especially the kitchen. She was in culinary school when Dad died. Hasn't had the urge to go back."

"Aw."

"She'll find her rhythm. She's heading up the bookstore's coffee shop project. That'll be in operation by Christmas."

"You guys really are a unit."

"We are now. When we were kids, Adam and I regularly tried to kill each other. Mila and Claudie got into it pretty good, too, but Tracy was around to mediate. Adam and I would sneak off somewhere and duke it out until we drew blood."

"Did that make the dunking booth fun?"

"Not really. Everyone expects me to dunk him so I play along. I'd give my life for Adam. He'd do the same for me."

Her throat tightened. She and Cole had a bond like that, but her career choice kept her from seeing him much. "I never thought about it before, but I'd give my life for Cole and he would for me."

"He must be a stand-up guy."

"The best."

"Are your parents still alive?"

"Yep."

"I just wondered since you don't—"

"They did their duty by us. We had food, clothes, a roof over our heads. But they weren't happy about it."

"What makes you say that?"

She shrugged. "They've always acted like we're this burden they've had to put up with. When we were little, Cole and I decided they'd been forced to take us because our real parents had been close relatives who'd died in a tragic accident."

"Logical."

"Cole wouldn't ask but when I was eleven I finally did. Mom showed me the birth certificates. We're theirs. So then I asked her if we'd been unplanned. She made a face and said *pretty much.*"

"Ouch." He took a breath. "I'm sorry. That sucks."

"Like I said, my family is nothing like yours. Which is why we need to really consider what we're doing with this... this *thing* that's brewing between us. Your family is being incredibly nice to me. I'm not going to repay that generosity by sneaking over to your casita in the middle of the night."

He met that with a snort of laughter.

"It's not funny, damn it!"

"It is, *querida.* You wouldn't say it if you hadn't already pictured yourself doing it. You don't even know how far you'd have to sneak. It's a big ranch."

Her face heated. He was right. That scenario had been running through her mind the entire time he'd been describing the ranch's layout. They wouldn't build those houses miles from each other, would they? Walking distance made more sense.

"FYI, it's about three—"

"Miles? Yikes. No way."

"Minutes."

"Oh." Her skin tingled. "So what? I'm not doing it." From the corner of her eye she caught his smile and the irresistible dimple that turned her inside out. "And no fair calling me *querida.*"

"No fair coming to Mustang Valley looking even more beautiful than you did five years ago." His voice softened. "I couldn't resist you then. How am I supposed to do it now?"

Those words, cloaked in the velvet tones she remembered all too well, sent shivers of arousal through her eager body. She could fight those urges now because she had her horse to think of.

But tonight, when Fudge had been treated and placed in a cozy stall, her horse wouldn't need her attention. And paradise would be only three minutes away.

9

Jordan fell silent after that. Could be a result of the heavier traffic they encountered as they drew closer to Missoula. But Luis figured she was chewing on his last comment, trying to frame a response and coming up empty.

He couldn't say when he'd gone all in. Might have been when he'd climbed into her truck and buckled up. After their first night together at the motel where they'd each booked a room, she'd cancelled hers and moved in with him.

He'd refused to let her pay half, so she'd insisted on driving them back and forth from the motel to the ranch where the clinic was held. Now he understood why that had mattered so much to her.

Today she was driving a newer, fancier truck and the situation wasn't the same at all. But riding shotgun with her in this cozy cab, where he could easily reach over and lay a hand on her thigh, had opened the floodgates. Hot memories swept him right past the warning lights of caution.

Of course he still had a choice. So did she. She had a will of iron forged by her parents' neglect.

She could be strong enough to stay in her room. In that case, he'd be taking a lot of cold showers.

But if she made that three-minute walk, game over. He'd welcome her with open arms and worry about fallout later.

As the string of businesses along the highway became more numerous, Jordan moved to the right lane and took the next exit. A couple of miles along that road the commercial sector gave way to rural countryside.

She broke the silence. "We're almost there. This shouldn't take too long. My trailer's parked next to the barn."

"How do you like the gooseneck?"

"Love it. I started out with a bumper hitch. When I could afford it, I traded it in for this gooseneck. There's so much less wobble with the connection in my truck bed."

"Agreed. That's all we've ever had at Laughing Creek."

"I've never dealt with a hoof abscess. Assuming that's what's wrong with Fudge, do you have any idea how long it takes to heal?"

"Monty can tell you better than I can, but it's probably several days. I doubt he'll be over it by Monday, if that's what you're asking."

"Yeah, I just realized that. I'll ask Monty to teach me how to care for him since I'll need to get back on the road by then. I'll borrow one of the horses at the venue for demonstrations. Fudge shouldn't be ridden until he's completely over it. I know that much."

"When's the clinic?" He'd seen her schedule on her website, but that had been weeks ago.

"Starts Thursday in Bozeman. I scheduled a few private sessions ahead of the event, so I really need to take off on Monday."

Bozeman was so damn close. He couldn't resist tossing out an idea. "How about leaving Fudge at Laughing Creek so Monty can keep an eye on him? Then you can fetch him when you're done." The minute the words were out of his mouth, the atmosphere in the truck changed.

"I wouldn't dream of imposing on Monty and your family like that."

"What if it's the best thing for Fudge?"

She gave him a look that clearly said *back off*.

But it was a logical plan, damn it. She could probably handle Fudge's care, but this would be easier on her and her horse. He opened his mouth to say so.

"Luis, don't."

"I'm only—"

"Be honest. Is this really about Fudge?"

"Of course it is."

"Would you swear to that?"

With a groan he closed his eyes and leaned back against the headrest. *Dios mio.* He'd blown it. "No. It's not entirely about him."

"Déjà vu all over again."

"Forget I said anything."

"This is why I didn't give you my phone number five years ago."

He grimaced. "The guardrails remain in place. I still don't have your phone number." She didn't have one listed on her website, just an email.

"Look, we're crazy about each other. That scares me."

Opening his eyes, he looked over at her. "Scares me a little, too."

"I've got this clinic thing grooved in. I don't know if you noticed on my website, but I have gigs in Texas, Arizona and New Mexico. It's the second winter in a row."

"I saw you'd expanded your territory. Congratulations."

"I've even talked to folks in Australia and New Zealand."

"That would be amazing." Made his gut clench to think of her that far away. He made a mental note to never look at her schedule.

"I'll get there. I know I will as long as I stay focused."

"Message received." He'd seen an opportunity to keep her within reach for a few more days and he'd blindly grabbed onto it. He hadn't acknowledged his hidden agenda until she'd called him on it.

In the process he might have ruined any chance she'd pay that visit to his casita. If he'd screwed that up, maybe it was for the best.

"We're here." She turned down a paved road bordered by a rustic fence. They passed a large arena similar to the one at the clinic where they'd met.

Nice facility. "How many did you have last weekend?"

"Twenty-four."

"Impressive."

"It was a good turnout. I always cap attendance at thirty, and a few times I've had to put folks on a waiting list."

"That's a good sign. Clearly folks are excited about your clinics."

"Yeah." There was a smile in her voice. "They are."

His chest warmed. Confidence looked great on her. He wanted her to be a success. She had a lot of talent and she was making use of it.

She was justifiably proud of what she'd accomplished and the life she'd created. He'd keep that knowledge front and center from now on. Eventually he'd get used to the bittersweet taste.

When he glimpsed her sleek white gooseneck trailer, he let out a whistle of surprise. "You travel in style, lady."

"Took a while to pay it off, but I kept reminding myself that I was saving the money I would have spent on a motel room and Fudge has better quarters than he had with the old trailer."

"Speaking of Fudge, once you get the truck lined up, I'd be glad to do the hitching if you want to fetch him and settle your bill."

She hesitated a fraction of a second. "Okay, that would save time. Thank you."

"You're welcome."

"I've never trusted anyone to hitch up my trailer before."

"I fully believe that and I'm honored to be the first."

"But a bystander can be helpful for unlatching the tailgate and guiding me into position."

"I'm happy to be today's bystander."

"Thanks."

The lilt in her voice reminded him of the way they'd teased each other five years ago. The light mood had lasted right up to the final couple of hours.

Until then, he hadn't believed they'd go their separate ways. He'd learned his lesson. Evidently he'd have to relearn it.

Pulling into the complex, she swung her truck around, backed toward the trailer and stopped a couple feet away. "You're up."

"I'm on it." He climbed out, lowered the tailgate and raised the coupler on the gooseneck. Her trailer was a beauty. Once they'd returned to Laughing Creek and Fudge had been doctored, he'd ask for a tour of the living quarters.

Stepping away, he guided Jordan as she backed into position. "A little to the left *por favor.* A little more. *Bueno!*"

She shut off the engine, hopped out and grabbed her backpack from behind the seat. "I'll get Fudge."

He'd expected her to come check on the hitch's position before she left him with this assignment. "Want to make sure you're lined up right?"

She held his gaze. "I do, but I'm not going to."

"Okay, then." Her earnest expression was touching. Trust was so hard for her.

"Thanks again." Hoisting the backpack over her shoulder, she turned and started toward the barn.

"Anytime." She likely hadn't heard him.

Didn't matter. It was a pointless response. He'd never get the chance to do this again. With so many vehicles at the ranch she'd have no reason to use her truck. She could leave it hitched to the trailer.

When she performed this maneuver again, she'd be on her own. Far away from him. That's how she wanted it.

But he was here now, and he'd give her the best damn hitching job in existence. He made sure everything was tight, secure, *perfecto*. He hooked up the lights, confirmed they were working and then went over everything again before closing the tailgate.

By the time he'd finished setting up the ramp, Jordan was coming around the corner of the barn with her decidedly lame horse. Fudge's head hung down, almost as if he needed to study the terrain and avoid any hazards.

Luis winced. "Looks painful."

"I'm sure it is, poor guy. Jeb showed me what he thinks is the abscess and it looks nasty. I wondered if I'd somehow missed that Fudge had a problem, but he said abscesses really can happen overnight."

"They can." He pulled out his phone. "Let's get the image for Monty and then tuck him in so we can get on the road."

"Actually, I took a picture while Jeb was showing me his hoof." She slipped her backpack off her shoulder.

"Great. Text it to me and...." If she did that, he'd have her number. "Or you can text it straight to Monty."

"Makes more sense." She didn't look at him as she looped Fudge's lead rope around her arm and dug out her phone.

"Right." He pulled up Monty's number and read it to her. Now Monty would have her digits. Whoever said life was fair?

"Done." She put her phone away and walked the gelding around to the ramp. In the shade he was coal black, not a speck of white, but in the sun his coat took on a cocoa brown tinge, justifying his name.

She stroked his glossy neck. "Go on in, sweet boy. We'll get you fixed up as soon as we can."

Fudge seemed eager to get inside the trailer, which likely felt like home to him. But he grunted in pain whenever he accidentally put weight on his injured hoof.

Stowing the ramp, Jordan closed and latched the trailer's doors. "This is awful. He's always been so healthy. I hate that he's hurting."

"He won't have to be in pain much longer. Let's do this." He lengthened his stride as he headed for the truck's passenger side.

Jordan must have jogged around to her side. She was seated and buckled up by the time he got in and closed the door. He quickly fastened his seat belt as she started the engine.

She took a quick breath. "I can't decide whether to take it slow to make sure I don't jostle him or go fast so we'll get there sooner."

"Your horse, your call."

"What would you do?"

Her question surprised him. "I'd put myself in Fudge's shoes. I think he'd want you to take it easy so you can watch for anything in the road. His balance won't be great right now. He'll have anxiety about that."

She nodded. "I'll go slow." Checking all her mirrors, she maneuvered carefully out of the complex. Once they were back on the 90, she let out a heavy sigh.

He knew what it was like to have a beloved horse in pain. "You're doing great."

She kept her attention on the road. "I'm glad you came along."

"Me, too."

"Which makes it even more important that I leave on Monday. I could get used to having you around."

"Same." Clearly their growing connection scared the stuffing out of her. Scared him, too. But he craved it more than his next breath.

10

Jordan enjoyed driving solo, which was a good thing because she did a ton of it. That said, Luis made an excellent traveling companion.

Conversation came easily, just as it had five years ago. Or maybe he was making a concerted effort to keep her mind off her injured horse.

That was entirely possible, especially since he focused on a topic guaranteed to keep her engaged — her work. He had questions, lots of them, regarding how she structured the lessons and where she placed the emphasis.

She explained what she'd adapted from the clinics she'd attended and where she'd chosen to innovate. Discussing it with him energized her. She and Luis approached the subject of horse behavior with the same respect and empathy. She didn't find that often.

In fact, almost never. Luis's intuitive understanding of animals, especially horses, was rare. She might have noticed the same ability in Spence Bridger if she'd been lucky enough to have met him.

About thirty minutes into the drive back to Mustang Valley, Luis called Monty. Their conversation was brief. After he disconnected, he tucked his phone away. "He'll be there to meet us."

"Good. I still hate pulling him away from the celebration, but after seeing what Fudge is going through...."

"Like I said, Monty prioritizes a sick animal over just about anything else. He's been like that since he was a kid. He'd bring home some half-dead critter we all assumed was a goner, but soon that squirrel or bird or rabbit would be fully recovered ready to live *la buena vida*."

"Mila's diary on the H&H website talks about him a lot. It sounds like he has his hands full treating the wild horses. On the job 24/7."

"That's about right. Luckily there's another equine vet in town, because plenty of folks have horses. Noelle's busy, too, but when Monty gets slammed, she'll often volunteer her time to help."

"And on the one day he takes time off, here I am with—"

"You need to let go of that."

"You're right. It is what it is."

"Just remember what I said about him. Riding to the rescue is his thing."

"I'll keep that in mind. It seems like a theme around here. Everyone's friendly and helpful, both to strangers and each other."

"Mostly. We have some feuds going on, though. Auntie Kat and Eli Hawthorne, for example."

"Eli, the leader of the Polar Bear Club?"

"How do you know that?"

"I passed their wagon on my way to the staging area to wait for you. He invited me to ride in the wagon with them."

Luis chuckled. "Color me surprised."

"At the H&H gathering I got more info from Kat. Is she really a member of their club?"

"Only to irritate Eli. Or so she says. We all think they might be bitter enemies in public and something else in private, but we have no proof."

"I love it. Romantic intrigue, elder style. What's more fun than that?"

"I can think of a few things, *querida*."

No mystery as to what he was referring to, especially the way he'd said it. "Are you doing that on purpose?"

"Doing what?"

"Using your super sexy voice to turn me on."

He grinned. "I wasn't aware my voice had that kind of power."

"Aw, c'mon. You know you do it."

"I don't know that at all. Enlighten me."

"You drop down a register and your voice takes on a velvety quality, especially when you throw in some Spanish."

"Velvety?"

"It's very effective."

"I swear it's unconscious, but thanks for letting me know I have a secret weapon." He lowered his voice to a husky purr and gave her a heavy-lidded stare. "*Eres hermosa y te quiero.*"

She grinned. "I assume that's your smolder."

"Depends. Did it work?"

"Not when you lay it on thick like that. Subtle is better. Besides, I have no idea what you said. For all I know it was *I'd like a burrito and two tacos to go.*"

"Nope."

"Then what did you say?"

"Does it matter? It sounds like it's the delivery more than the content."

"It's both, so since I don't know what those words mean, it loses steam."

"I said you're beautiful... and I want you." Sensuality flowed through every syllable.

She went up in flames. "Oh."

"Which you are and I do, despite trying my damnedest not to."

"We... um... should probably change the subject."

"Don't blame me. You're the one who said my voice turned you on."

"We went off the rails when you told me about Kat and Eli getting frisky."

"Well, since we're off the rails—"

"We need to get back on them."

"Okay, but first let me say something."

"Or not." Her heart thumped faster.

"We won't have this kind of privacy once we get to the ranch. I know you have objections to spending the night—"

"Seriously, let's not discuss it now."

"But if you decide to, you'll be welcome."

She swallowed. Maybe they should hash it out before they arrived. "Spending the night could make you want to change things."

"No, it won't. I get it. Seeing that venue and hearing about your program made me a believer. I understand what it means to you. My body wants what it wants, but my head knows you need to leave on Monday. I'm not the one for you. End of story."

"What if I lose your family's good opinion?"

"They don't have to know. You could slip out and back in undetected. But even if they find out, they won't judge."

She let out a breath. "Then why were you so reluctant to say anything about you and me?"

"I wasn't afraid of being judged. I just didn't want to face a bunch of questions. I didn't say they wouldn't be curious. But—" His phone chimed. "That'll be Monty." He put his phone to his ear.

His side of the conversation indicated that Monty had studied the photo and agreed with Jeb. Luis confirmed it after he hung up. "He's got a stall prepped. He's ready for him."

"That's awesome."

"At the next intersection, go right. That will take you to Laughing Creek. We're almost there."

"Got it." She made the turn onto a deserted two-lane. They'd encountered very little traffic in the last half-hour or so, likely because everyone had made it to wherever they'd spend the rest of the day and evening.

Before this development with Fudge, she'd looked forward to seeing her first Fourth of July laser show. She no longer cared about that, but she hoped Monty would finish up in time to go back to town.

"The next right will be it."

She put on her turn signal even though there was no one to see it. Anticipation bubbled up within her, despite her worry about Fudge. Luis had described the ranch in loving detail. Now she'd see for herself what— *oh, my goodness.*

The massive wrought iron gate featured a metal version of the same black horse that was on her shirt, the running mustang that Zay had made into a 3-D version for the H&H parade wagon. "What a spectacular entryway."

"Sure is. By the way, the gate's automatic. Pull up to the keypad post. The code's 0714, Mom's birthday."

Pulling over to the left, she rolled down the window and tapped in the code. The gate slowly opened and she drove through, checking in the rearview mirror to make sure the trailer cleared before the gate closed again. "That code's a lovely way to honor your mom."

"It's more of a family joke. Dad loved the idea of automated gates. She reluctantly agreed to this one because it was a good way to keep the wild horses in, but then he wanted to put them everywhere and she was so against it. Thought it would make us all lazy."

"And?"

"He finally wore her down and we have automated gates everywhere, all with the same code, which gives you a taste of his sense of humor. Now the gates remind her of him and she loves them."

"That's touching."

"Reminds the rest of us, too, but then almost everything on the ranch does that."

"Is the wire fence on either side of the gate electric?"

"It is. One of our biggest expenses, but without it, we have no sanctuary for the horses."

"I had a mental picture from looking at the website and reading Mila's diary, but seeing it in person is so much better."

"Glad you came?"

"That's a complicated question." A white fence now lined the road to their left and eventually they came to another gate with a fancy LCR at the top. Sure enough, it had a keypad post, too.

"Why is it a complicated question?"

"There are so many aspects to this visit." She tapped in the code and pulled through.

"There are multiple aspects to working with a troubled horse. You deal with them the same way I do, one at a time as they present themselves."

"This isn't even remotely the same."

"Sure it is. Right now we're going to get Fudge some help. Then we'll see where we are."

"You're saying I should go with the flow. Just because I can do that when I'm working with a horse doesn't mean I'm comfortable taking that approach to my life."

"Are you comfortable trying to control all the aspects of this visit?"

"Of course not, but—"

"Then what have you got to lose?"

She knew the answer to that one.

Myself.

_11_

Luis had never been so glad that Monty had decided to become a vet. His brother's calm, capable handling of Fudge's issue soothed the horse and Jordan.

The abscess was draining. Fudge had a massive bandage on his right foreleg which he kept eyeing with suspicion. But he was no longer grunting in pain and was extremely interested in his hay flake and a bucket of oats.

Jordan was all smiles, and wasn't that great to see? Monty was happy, too. He lived for moments like this.

The barn was quiet. After the parade, they'd filled the slow feeder in the pasture and turned all the horses out to enjoy themselves. This time of year was perfect grazing weather.

Now that the emergency was handled, he was hungrier than a grizzly coming out of hibernation. "Who's ready to eat?"

"Not me." Monty leaned against the side of the stall watching Fudge nose through the bucket of oats. "I filled up on barbeque before I left town."

Jordan laughed. "I wasn't hungry until you mentioned barbeque. Now I'm starving."

"You two go find some grub in Luis's kitchen." Monty made a shooing motion with his hand. "I'll keep an eye on our patient."

She frowned. "I hate to leave. Hey, Luis, could we throw something together and bring it back over here?"

"Sure. I'll do it. You don't have to go. I'll fetch us a couple of sandwiches."

Monty shook his head. "I really don't think you need to worry. Fudge is enjoying his meal. You go enjoy yours. Luis might even have some of Auntie Ezzie's tamales in his fridge."

"I do, and they're calling my name." He glanced at Jordan. "Are you a fan?"

"Homemade tamales? Are you kidding? I'm in. But I'd still like to bring my plate—"

"I don't want to stop you," Monty said, "But I predict by the time you get here your horse will be taking a nap. He had a rough night and he's exhausted. I guess you could eat and watch him sleep, but those tamales deserve a sit-down lunch."

Was Monty deliberately creating a chance for them to be alone in the casita? Luis wouldn't put it past him. He'd made his opinion known this morning.

"Well…" Jordan walked over to Fudge and gave him a scratch under his mane. "Hey, sweet boy. I'm gonna grab some chow. You take it easy, okay?"

Fudge lifted his head briefly, gave her a look and went back to his oats, which made her chuckle. "I think you're right, Monty. He doesn't need me hovering over him."

"Take your phone," Monty said. "If I have any concerns I'll call you."

Luis's jaw tightened. Monty couldn't know the significance of that innocent statement. Sure did underline the issue and add several exclamation marks, though, didn't it?

"Thanks. I'll grab it on the way over." She left the barn and he followed her around to the side where she'd parked her truck and trailer.

She opened the driver's door. "This must chap your hide."

"What?" Maybe she'd believe he was unfazed.

"You know what." She grabbed her backpack from behind the seat. "This is starting to feel stupid."

"Agreed."

Retrieving her phone, she returned the backpack to its spot, closed the door and faced him. "You're not going to sabotage me. You can have my number. If you still want it. I shouldn't make assumptions."

"I do still want it." He pulled his phone from his hip pocket. "I won't use it, but I want it."

"If you're not going to use it, then why—"

"Because when you call me, I'll know who it is. I won't delete it as junk."

"But I'm not planning on calling you."

"Then I guess we won't be speaking on the phone, because that's the only way it'll happen. You'll have to make the call."

She studied him. "I hurt you when I wouldn't exchange numbers."

"Dinged my pride a little. But you were smart not to five years ago. I would have used it. I would have pushed."

"And now you won't call me? Ever?"

"That's right."

"Not even if you're at death's door?"

He blinked. "Why would I call you? Are you moonlighting as a priest?"

She flushed and turned her attention to her phone. "I don't know what made me say that."

"Me, either. Never occurred to me I should have a list of folks to notify when I'm on the way out."

"It was a dumb comment. Forget it. What's your number?"

He gave it to her while mulling over her odd request. Wanting to know if he was alive or dead was a low bar for gauging affection. But he'd take it. "I doubt I'll croak anytime soon, but if that changes, I'll give you a jingle."

"Never mind."

"That's assuming I have my—" His phone chimed. He'd been expecting the ping of a text, but instead she'd opted for a call. He met her gaze. "Who's this and why are you calling me?"

That made her laugh. "My bad. I should have texted."

"Yes, ma'am, that's a fact. You specifically said you weren't planning to call me, and twenty seconds later, here you are, talking to me on the phone. What am I supposed to make of that?"

"That I'm not firing on all cylinders. This thing with Fudge has me discombobulated. A text would've made more sense."

"Oh, yeah, blame it on Fudge. By the way, you look cute in that H&H cap. I kept meaning to tell you so."

Color bloomed in her cheeks. "Thanks. You have my number, so we can hang up now."

"I hate to. This feels like a moment. Our first phone chat." And likely their one and only.

"While we're standing face-to-face. If anybody saw this they'd think we're a couple of nut jobs."

"They wouldn't be wrong."

"That's for sure. Okay, we really should say goodbye."

"I know, but I like hearing your voice in my ear."

The sparkle of laughter in her eyes became a soft glow he knew all too well. As that glow turned her blue eyes darker, her breathing changed.

Saliva pooled in his mouth and instinct took over, guiding his attention lower. Her H&H T-shirt was loose, but not loose enough to disguise the rapid rise and fall of her breasts.

He gripped his phone. As long as he held onto it, he wouldn't do something stupid, like backing her up against the truck and kissing the daylights out of her.

Lifting his gaze, he met the heat in hers. No help there. If he made a move, she wouldn't stop him.

A throbbing ache taunted him, tested him. Had it been this way before? Or had time added layers of need? "*Querida*...."

She gulped. "Goodbye, Luis." Lowering her phone, she broke eye contact, disconnected and stepped away from the truck. "I don't think... maybe I shouldn't come in with you."

He sucked in air. "Right. I have an umbrella table..." *Breathe, boy, breathe.* "On the patio."

"I was gonna help."

"Yeah. Not necessary." He had no trouble picturing what would happen the minute they walked through his arched front doorway. They'd skip the kitchen entirely.

"You said the patio has a wall?"

"Waist-high."

"Ah. Good."

"We'll be fine. Let's go." Easier said than done. Pocketing his phone would tighten the fit of his already painfully snug jeans so he held onto it. He winced as he took the first step.

"We don't have to rush over there."

He snorted. "Thanks. Appreciate it." Clenching his jaw, he started off. Slowly.

"Believe me, if I'd known you were unattached...."

"You wouldn't have come?"

"Tough call. The sanctuary tour and the book signing really appealed to me. But I would've—"

"Prevented Fudge's abscess?"

She sighed. "Good point."

"You'd have ended up here one way or the other. Like I said. Inevitable."

"That doesn't mean we're destined to end up in bed."

"Totally up to you. You know what I think about it."

"Was Monty trying to help things along?"

"Could be. He can't imagine why we wouldn't avail ourselves of the opportunity. I tend to agree with him. Riding in your truck brought back a ton of memories."

"You used to reach over and squeeze my thigh."

"Couldn't keep my hands off you. Good thing the clinic was intense. No time for fooling around."

"But we made up for it later."

"Yes, ma'am. That's why we'll be eating lunch outside."

"I see two casitas ahead. Which one is yours?

"The second one. Red umbrella. You might want to take note of that so you don't walk in on Zay."

"You sound pretty sure of yourself."

"I wasn't until I saw that look in your eyes just now."

"That phone call should have been silly, but instead...."

"It doesn't take much."

"Especially when we're alone. But tonight, when your whole family is back here, that will make a huge difference. Once I'm tucked into my room at the main house, I'll find the inner strength to stay there."

He chuckled. "Keep telling yourself that."

_12_

The delicious aroma of warm masa and fragrant chili peppers drifted through the open windows of Luis's dun-colored casita. Jordan settled deeper into one of four cushy chairs ringing a wrought-iron table.

She'd deliberately inserted herself into this colorful, tempting world. Luis's world. No point in blaming anyone or anything for the war going on in her mind and body. She'd created it.

Before Luis had gone inside, he'd tilted the red umbrella to provide rose-tinted shade. Then he'd made tracks for his kitchen.

What did it look like? She wouldn't find out unless she crept over here tonight. Her internal debate began all over again.

This cozy domestic setting didn't surprise her. It suited him. But unlike her, he wasn't meant to live alone. She'd known that from the get-go. Why in hell wasn't he married by now?

While moving around in the kitchen, he began humming _Cielito Lindo_. He called it his theme song. She couldn't hear it without remembering their last night together.

He'd sung it to her and then translated the lyrics. The inspiring message—*sing, don't cry*—was how he wanted to live his life.

That intimate detail was only one of many he'd shared with her during those three days and passion-filled nights. Why?

She'd been too young and self-absorbed to ask herself that question. But now that she'd spent time with him on his own turf, the answer was obvious.

He'd been raised surrounded by a loving family and a supportive community. When he found a kindred spirit, he was hard-wired to make a deep connection.

Today he'd claimed to have seen the light. They weren't meant to be. End of story. How had he put it? *My body wants what it wants, but my head knows you have to leave on Monday.*

Sounded good, didn't it? Logical. Except he'd left out a third, crucial element, one that governed both his head and his body.

She would take that into account during those times when his soulful brown eyes threatened to destroy her resistance. Whether she surrendered or stayed strong, she would drive away on Monday and she didn't want to leave a path of destruction in her wake.

"Hey, Jordan, *quieres una cervesa?*" he called through the window.

"*Si, por favor.*" A cold beer sounded awesome right now. He'd likely have stocked his favorite, Modelo.

She hadn't tasted that hearty brew in five years. It would go great with tamales and if alcohol lowered their defenses a wee bit, the lack of privacy would keep them in check.

Moments later, the arched wooden door swung open and Luis appeared, balancing a loaded wooden tray with one hand while he closed the door with the other. He'd left his hat inside. "Lunch is served."

"Wow." Damn, he was gorgeous. She itched to shove her fingers through those thick curls. She hoped he'd assume she'd exclaimed over the tray of food and not the hunk of burning love delivering it.

She stood. "Let me help you with that."

"No worries." He laid out two placemats and added napkins and silverware. "I'm a professional. Don't try this at home."

"Clearly somebody used to wait tables." She returned to her seat, flushed with the battle between lust and logic. His rolled-up sleeves drew her gaze to his muscled forearms and his strong, capable hands as he deposited a frosty bottle of dark beer at each place.

"We all worked as servers. Mom and Dad encouraged us to get a job at least one summer at the Raccoon. They said it builds character."

"I agree with that." He'd earned a few more scars since she'd last seen him. Wrangling horses, especially wild ones, meant getting scraped up. But it was good work, humane work, and he'd dedicated his life to it. Admirable. Sexy as hell.

"Being a server was fun most of the time." The sky-blue pottery plate he put in front of her held three wrapped tamales and a generous helping of refried beans. "But there's always that one entitled customer."

"And they're the ones who don't tip."

"Yes, ma'am." He took his seat. "We'd come home complaining about it, and Dad would say *just remember it sucks to be them.*"

"What a great response." She surveyed the feast he'd laid before her. "And what a great lunch! Thanks so much. You're spoiling me."

"*Con gusto, senorita.*"

My pleasure. Her skin tingled. Did he remember saying that whenever she'd thanked him for an amazing time in bed?

She made the mistake of glancing up. Oh, yeah, he remembered. The simmering heat and subtle invitation in his dark eyes combined with that dimpled smile created havoc in her lady parts.

She should have kept her focus on her plate. Now she couldn't see anything but her dream lover and the arched doorway over his right shoulder. Who cared about tamales?

"I'd forgotten." His soft murmur deepened the spell. "When you want me, you glow."

"It's the red umbrella."

"It's not the umbrella. It's you. It's us."

She struggled to breathe. "We can't...."

"No, we can't." His voice grew husky. "But I want to. So do you."

She had no response. He was right.

Holding her gaze, he reached for his beer.

Then she remembered something else. They used to toast some random thing before taking their first sip. Nothing noble or sentimental. Silly stuff. She picked up her bottle, the chilled glass sending a shiver through her overstimulated body.

He cleared his throat. "To Fudge's right front hoof."

Worked for her. "To Fudge's right front hoof." She tapped her bottle against his and took a sip.

He chose differently. Lifting the bottle to his lips, he tilted his head back and closed his eyes as he took several long swallows.

She couldn't look away. The blatant sensuality of that move sent her pulse into overdrive and dampened her panties.

Setting the bottle down with a sigh, he picked up one of the corn-husk-wrapped tamales. "Be careful with these. They're super-hot."

"Thanks." The tamales weren't the only super-hot thing around here. She took another sip of her beer to steady her nerves. Then she carefully unwrapped a tamale and picked up a fork. "You must have been thirsty."

His soft chuckle sent another shudder of longing through her. "Oh, I was. Still am."

"Damn it, Luis."

"I just responded to your comment."

"You also confirmed that you knew exactly what you were doing, drinking like you were making love to the bottle."

"It was either that or kiss you. We both know what would happen next. Monty wouldn't say anything if we were gone a couple of hours, but I predict you'd be awash in guilt."

"A couple of hours?" That image made her shake so bad she put down her fork.

"At least." He hadn't even picked up his. "It's been five years." The gleam in his eyes held her captive. "We have a lot of catching up to do."

His assumption that it was a done deal challenged her to push back. "Or not. I haven't agreed to anything."

"I can see you're fighting this tooth and nail, but it's like they say in the movies." He smiled. "This is bigger than both of us."

"What is?"

"Circumstances. Fate. We didn't choose to be thrown together, but—"

"I did. I chose it."

"Yeah, the trip was your idea, but you didn't choose Fudge's problem. That's the key to it, right there."

"Is that why you toasted his right front hoof?"

"Yes, ma'am. I would never wish any animal harm, but since I had nothing to do with his issue, I'm willing to accept the gift that came with it." He picked up his beer again. "Are you?"

Not if she would do damage. She hesitated, then forged ahead. "What if I hurt you?"

An emotion flickered in his eyes. Then it was gone and his dimples flashed as he smiled. "You just might. As I recall, you're quite the tiger in bed. I'll take my chances."

"Luis, I'm serious. What if—"

"Let me worry about that." He took a gulp of beer and set the bottle down with a decisive click. "If you want to have some fun this weekend, but you're afraid you'll leave me a broken man...."

He met her gaze. "I promise that will not be the case."

She stared at him, heart thumping. "How can you make that promise?"

"Easy. My family. Come hell or high water, they've got me. On the other hand, you're on your own. If you're liable to end up worse off emotionally, then we're done talking about it."

She took a quick breath. "I can take care of myself."

"Then will I see you later tonight?"

She'd warned him and he'd shrugged it off. At this point she'd make his life difficult no matter what she decided. So maybe—

"It would be nice to know in advance."

"Oh. I suppose you'll need to pick up some—"

"I have those. But if I know you're coming over, I'll shower and shave. I'll put fresh sheets on the bed. I remember you enjoyed having clean ones each night at the motel."

"I did. I loved every minute of being with you in that room."

"Then let's do it all over again, *querida*."

She took a long, slow breath and let it out. He looked and sounded like the cowboy in her dream, but he hadn't said *we belong together.*

Mentally crossing her fingers, she met his gaze. "Okay."

13

Luis wanted to kiss Jordan more than he'd ever wanted to kiss her, and that was saying something. But once he touched down on those soft lips, clothes would be coming off.

He gazed at her. Should they? "I want to go inside."

"Me, too."

He tossed his napkin on the table.

"Don't get up!" She looked panicked. "You're right. I'll feel guilty about Fudge."

"We won't be gone two hours. I just said that to be a smartass. We'll set an alarm. We'll—"

"It's not only the time. Going back after... I'd feel weird. And what if something happens with Fudge? And Monty calls when we're—"

"Damn. Hadn't thought of that." He sighed and brought his chair back flush with the table. "I got carried away. Sorry."

"It's okay." Her smile was tender. "Anyway, we really should eat Auntie Ezzie's homemade tamales."

He grimaced. "Which are now getting cold."

"Not that cold." She took a bite of tamale and hummed with delight.

That sexy hum went straight to his groin, but too bad. He was the boss of his package. "Yeah, Auntie Ezzie knows what she's doing."

"She makes them by herself?"

"Oh, no." He welcomed the G-rated topic. Digging into his food, he began describing the communal tamale effort, a day-long process that resulted in a six-month supply for each of them.

Jordan had all kinds of questions just as she had whenever he'd talked about the ranch or his family five years ago. She might not want to live his life, but she certainly was fascinated by the details of it.

He controlled his temptation to flirt with her. Wasn't easy, but he needed to hone his *just friends* role for her benefit. Clearly she didn't want his family to know what they were up to.

Unfortunately, the Bridger Bunch had a talent for picking up on the slightest cue. They'd be looking, too, now that everybody knew the steamy backstory. But he wouldn't say any of that to Jordan.

She waited on the patio while he put the plates and utensils in the dishwasher. Grabbing his hat on the way out, he started to close the door. "Want to take a look inside? I'll stay out here."

She shook her head. "I don't want to see any of it, especially your bedroom. I'm too fixated on tonight as it is, without feeding significant details to my very active imagination."

"Understood. Let's go check on Fudge."

"Let's do." She started off.

Putting on his hat, he fell into step beside her. "I'm not gonna hold your hand."

"Didn't expect you to. Did we ever do that?"

"Come to think of it, no. We were either at the clinic, in your truck or in the motel room."

"No strolling around town."

"No, ma'am. I didn't have strolling on my mind."

She laughed. "Me, either."

That said, he wouldn't mind taking her hand as they walked back to the barn. But that behavior, especially in public, signaled a commitment. Didn't fit their arrangement.

"It's reassuring Monty hasn't called. I didn't ask about the plan going forward, though. I wonder how much Fudge will need to be monitored."

"I'm guessing not much. I watched him wrap that bandage and it's not going anywhere until it's time to change it in the morning. The way he was talking, it sounds like the best thing we can do for Fudge is leave him alone and let him rest while the abscess drains."

"I got that, too. Which is why I feel comfortable sending you two back to the festivities."

"You'd stay here?" He didn't like that idea at all.

"I think I should, just to keep an eye on him."

"You'll miss the laser show and dancing at the Raccoon."

"Fudge's well-being is more important."

"I agree. But if he's not in critical condition, then—"

"I'd just feel better. I'm his best friend, and next to Cole, he's mine, too."

"Then you need to stay." The unwelcome tightness in his chest was information he'd rather not receive. He was jealous of both her brother and her horse. How messed up was that?

"Thanks for understanding."

"I could keep you company."

She laughed. "There are so many ways that could go wrong."

"Or right. Ever done it in a barn?"

"No, and I'm certainly not starting with this one." She glanced over at him. "Have you?"

"No, ma'am."

"The way you asked the question, I assumed you were into it."

"I could be with the right person."

"I could be with the right barn."

"Smarty pants. Sure you don't want me to stay? We'd be discreet."

"Sorry. Wrong barn. And since we're almost there, we should talk about something else."

"If you stay here, what about your dinner?"

"I have plenty to eat in my trailer."

"That reminds me, will you show me the inside some time? Not now, but while you're here."

"Sure. In the daylight, with the door wide open."

He slapped a hand against his chest. "You wound me, dear lady. I would never—"

"And we need a new topic. Don't worry about me feeding myself. I've been doing it for years."

"Your parents didn't cook?"

"I guess you could call it that. Cole and I got so tired of feeling like a burden. Once he had a fast-food job, he moved out and rented a room. When I made enough to pay my share, we found a cheap apartment. Life was way better after that."

He was getting the picture and it wasn't a pretty one. She'd learned not to impose on anyone, not even her brother. Those two had likely split chores and money with absolute precision.

As they reached the barn he paused and waited for her to go in ahead of him. Then he stepped through the open door into cool shade.

When Jordan entered Fudge's stall, Monty rose from the upended bucket he'd used for a stool. He'd already packed up his med kit. Fudge lay on his side, eyes closed, his beathing steady.

He waited outside the stall as they talked in hushed tones. When he joined them, Jordan turned. "He's doing good."

"Glad to hear it."

Monty kept his voice down. "This is the best thing for him, a quiet stall, and no horses around so he can relax and recover."

"It's perfect," Jordan said. "He wouldn't have had anything like this if I'd used a vet in Missoula. I'm so grateful for what you've done. I'd like to pay—"

"It's on the house. You're a friend of the family."

"Luis said you wouldn't accept it." She glanced at him. "Guess I'll just have to make a big ol' donation to Hearts & Hooves."

Of course she would. He should have seen that coming. He liked his brother's *friend of the family* phrase, though. Might come in handy if he needed to introduce her to anyone.

Monty rubbed his chin where a five-o'clock shadow was beginning to show. "Well, I can't exactly stop you from doing that. We can always use it, but it's really not necessary."

"It is to me. So how long do you think he'll sleep?"

"Quite a while. I'm guessing at least six hours or more now that he's not in pain."

She nodded. "Since he's doing so well and will probably just sleep for a while, why don't you and Luis drive back to town? I'll stick around here."

Monty frowned and sent him a quick what-the-hell glance. "As far as I'm concerned, we can all leave. No reason for you to miss out."

"I'll feel better staying. That way I can alert you in case something should change."

"Ah. I must've forgotten to mention my spy system."

"Yeah, me too." Luis felt like a moron. Seemed to be a pattern with him today. His brother had been using security cameras for several months, now.

So much for the barn sex he'd fantasized. Monty moved those cameras all the time, depending on what he needed to monitor. They could be anywhere. Probably in this stall.

Sure enough, his brother pointed to a crossbeam above them. "While you two had lunch, I set up one of my nifty cameras."

"Oh!" Jordan looked up in surprise.

"I'll show you." He dug out his phone. "I love these things. I can check on any horses under my care no matter where I am. Sometimes I have three or four going at once." He tapped on the phone and turned it around so Jordan could see the screen.

"Whoa. That's awesome. It takes in the entire stall — Fudge and the three of us." Her eyes sparkled with amusement. "What a game-changer, huh, Luis?"

He gave her a tight smile. "Yes, ma'am."

"For damn sure." Monty raved on, so proud of his latest toy that he clearly didn't notice that exchange. "Watch this. I can zoom in, get up close and personal with my patient."

Joran studied the screen. "Amazing. The focus is so sharp you could count the hairs in Fudge's tail."

A slight tremble in her voice gave her away. She was working hard not to laugh since it would confuse the hell out of Monty.

"That sharpness is crucial. I can zoom in on sutures, dressings, you name it, and tell what's going on." Monty swiped the screen and the image disappeared. "This system delivers the goods. I'll snap a picture before we go for reference. That way I'll be able to tell if anything's changed. If the situation looks at all dicey, I'll head back."

Jordan cleared her throat. "How often do you check it?"

"Every thirty minutes. I'll set an alert so I don't forget. I'm not telling you what to do, but I'd hate for you to miss out on all the fun in town tonight."

"And her boots have never gone dancing." He couldn't resist throwing that in.

Monty tucked his phone away and looked down at Jordan's feet. "Nice fringe! Get Luis to request *Beat This Summer.* It's perfect for a fast two-stop and he's the best dancer in the family."

"Is that so?"

"He's exaggerating." Warmth crept up from his shirt collar. "We're all good at it. Mom and Dad had us dancing from the get-go."

"I didn't say the rest of us are bad. We can all play a decent game of baseball, too. Then there's you." He turned to Jordan. "Have I convinced you to come into town with us?"

She smiled. "You have."

"Then my work here is done." He grabbed his med kit. "I'm gonna head to my house and clean up before we leave. I'll meet you at the truck in ten." He walked out of the barn singing *I'm a Yankee Doodle Dandy.*

Jordan grinned. "You really didn't remember the place was bugged?"

"I did not. I don't use those things so I forget they're even there."

"I like your brother. He's great."

"Yeah, he is. And contrary to what he said, I'm not the best dancer. Mom and Dad... well, now my mom is." He shoved his hands in his pockets so he wouldn't reach for her. They should step outside but it was nice here in the cozy barn, even if they'd never make love in it.

"Monty's just proud of you. That's sweet."

"Are you okay dancing with me?"

"After that buildup I can't wait."

"I might be rusty. Haven't gone dancing lately."

"That makes two of us."

He gazed at her. The physical ache would soon force him to suggest they leave this barn before temptation got the better of him. "Sounds like you don't get out much." He shouldn't be happy about that, but he was.

She gave a little shrug. "I'm kinda particular about who I spend time with."

He couldn't help smiling. "That makes two of us." Peas in a pod. On the same wavelength. Maybe even soul mates.

He couldn't shake the idea that Fate had brought them back together for a reason. But were they meant for each other? Or were they supposed to learn how to let go?

<u>14</u>

One more second alone in this barn and Jordan would launch herself at Luis, camera or no camera. "Hey, you wanted a look inside my trailer. Let's do that while we wait for Monty."

"Good idea."

She turned toward her sleeping horse. "Keep up the good work, Fudge. I'll be back to check on you later." She walked out of the stall.

Luis followed her and latched the door.

"Should we close those doors?" She glanced back as they left the barn.

"It'll stay cooler if we don't. Fudge is safe. The electric fence keeps the wild horses in and predators out."

"I hadn't thought of that. If he had to get a hoof abscess, I'm glad it was now, when he has the perfect place to start the healing process." She headed toward the side of the barn where she'd parked the truck and trailer.

"It worked out well." He fell into step beside her. "You sure picked the right name for that horse. His coat looks exactly like fudge, especially in the sun."

"But that's not where the name came from."

"No?"

"First I wanted to name him after my brother Cole but I was going to spell it *C-o-a-l*."

"That's not bad, either."

"He thought it would be confusing, so we drove to the stable on a naming mission. At the time he was working to break his F-bomb habit. We were in the stall tossing around ideas while we groomed my unnamed horse when he stomped on Cole's foot. He yelled out *fu...dge*. Mission complete."

"That's funny."

"Especially since these days he totally uses it to replace his favorite swear word. Once he came out with *How the fudge is Fudge?*"

Luis chuckled. "On purpose?"

"Oh, no. But it is now. It's a thing." She pulled down the steps before unlocking and opening the door to her living quarters. "Go on in. I'll watch for Monty." Coming back down the steps, she positioned herself so she could see Adam's truck parked in front of the barn.

"Thanks." He took off his hat and ducked through the door. "Smells nice in here."

"Probably my shampoo." She'd showered and washed her hair before closing up the trailer and driving down here Thursday. She'd never had a spacious bathroom, so adapting to this one had been easy.

"Sure is neat. Like you were expecting company."

"I always leave it like that. Let a small space get messy and it feels like you're in hell. At least for me." She didn't hate having him explore her space. Interesting. She'd thought she might.

This rig was special, purchased after she'd split with her wannabe partner and traded in her bumper-pull trailer. Her brother was the only one besides her who'd stepped inside until now.

Cole called it her turtle shell. He would know. His cozy apartment served as his. Loners-R-Us.

She'd had friends in school, but hadn't let them get too close. If you went to a sleepover you were supposed to host a sleepover.

She'd dared it once, and her parents' consent had been grudging. What had followed was a litany of complaints, many in front of her guests.

Cole had been her one constant, her North Star, and now she rarely saw him. Her clinics provided plenty of human contact, though. Conducting one provided an unambiguous fifty-fifty agreement. Clients paid and she gave them their money's worth.

She enjoyed interacting with them and repeat customers became friends. To a point. They'd meet for dinner at the local watering hole, but if they offered to buy her a meal or even a beer, she'd politely decline.

"Thought I'd lost you guys."

She jumped as Monty came around the corner. "I was supposed to watch for you." Consumed by the voices in her head, she'd unconsciously moved closer to the trailer, closer to Luis. "I got distracted and forgot."

"Where's my brother?"

"Right here." He appeared in the doorway and climbed down. "I asked for a look inside. It's nice. I expected it to be claustrophobic, but I didn't get that feeling at all." He put on his hat.

"They've come a long way with these rigs."

Jordan looked over at Monty. "Want to take a peek?" She surprised herself with the offer.

But maybe it wasn't so out of character. He'd just spent more than two hours ministering to her sick horse. If she could trust him with Fudge she could certainly allow him into her private sanctuary.

"I would like to see it. Never been inside one this fancy before." Removing his hat, he went up the steps and through the open door. Moments later he whistled in approval. "Sweet. Is that a queen?"

"Yep." She glanced at Luis. "You liked it, then?"

"A little too much." He lowered his voice. "I started picturing the fun you and I could have on that bed. Had to get the hell out of there."

Heat sluiced through her. "Thanks a bunch. Now I'm picturing us in there."

"I'd suggest we switch venues except my king's bigger. More room to play."

She took a deep breath and gazed up at the cloudless sky. "Could we please talk about something else?"

"Sorry, not sorry. It's all I can think about. And it's only a little past five. We have hours before—"

"Woo-ee, you've got all you need in here!" Monty's voice was muffled. "Fridge, stovetop, flat screen, tons of storage." He came back out, all smiles. "Now I wish I had a use for one of these."

His enthusiasm tickled her. It also helped put out the fire Luis had created. "If you ever want one, let me know. I can get you a deal." She started to lock up and changed her mind. No reason to while she was on the ranch.

"Maybe in my golden years. Like when the kids I haven't had yet can take over while my yet-to-be-discovered wife and I hit the road with our horses, which haven't been born yet, either. That's when you can expect a call."

"I look forward to it." Would she still be in touch with the Bridger Bunch then? Something about the solidarity of this ranch and its mission in life told her she might be. What a concept.

Monty settled his hat back on his head. "We should go. Claudie pinged me a while ago wanting an update. I told her we'd be leaving here soon." He made tracks for Adam's truck. "Luis, why don't you drive? Keys are in the ignition. I'll take the back seat."

"Looking for some shuteye?"

"Not a bad idea. Could be a late night at the Raccoon."

"Then go ahead and stretch out, old man. I'll be sure and avoid the potholes so I don't disturb your rest."

"Don't tease the poor guy. He worked hard on Fudge." She took Luis's hand as he helped her into the front passenger seat.

First contact. The warmth of his firm grip traveled to every nerve in her body. She didn't dare look at him. "Thanks."

"My pleasure."

She gulped. He'd said it on purpose. She just knew it. Now she was flushed and struggling with the seatbelt.

Monty climbed into the back seat and leaned forward. "Need help?"

"It's okay. I've got it." She shoved the tongue into the buckle. She'd have to be cooler than this once they rejoined the rest of the Bridger Bunch.

Luis swung up behind the wheel, closed his door and buckled up. When he started the engine, Kenny Chesney's *Take Her Home* blasted from the speakers. He turned it down. "Way to break our eardrums, *hermano.*"

"I like it loud when I'm alone. Keeps me from dozing off. That's also a good tune by the way. You could request that one tonight for a two-step."

"We just might." Luis flicked a glance her way. "We'll see how it goes." Putting the truck in reverse, he backed around and drove slowly out of the yard to the paved road they'd come in on.

He looked good behind the wheel. Adam's truck had enough headroom that he'd left his hat on. Since she'd driven them back and forth from the motel five years ago, she'd never ridden in his truck, never seen him drive.

Too bad for her, that turned her on, too. Desperate to change her focus, she swiveled in her seat and looked back at Monty. "Thanks again for sacrificing a big chunk of your party time for my horse."

He settled back in the seat. "You're very welcome. Any day I can help an animal in trouble is a good day. It's the reason I get up in the morning."

Luis glanced at her. "Told you."

"Well, I'm grateful that you were so willing to help Fudge." She couldn't decide if he really wanted to sleep or had made that up so she and Luis could sit together in front. "Were you kidding about taking a nap?"

"No, ma'am. I get drowsy in a moving vehicle. I'm told when I was a baby that was the only way they could get me to sleep. It still works."

"Then I'll quit bending your ear."

"You're welcome to bend mine." Luis grinned. He and Monty were both developing a bit of stubble. Monty's was a lighter color and didn't show much. Luis's beard was darker, making him look rakish.

As Monty leaned back and tilted his hat down over his face, she turned to Luis. "Okay, what gets you up in the morning?"

His grin widened. The devil.

"Hey."

He lowered his voice. "Like I said, I have a one-track mind."

She took a deep breath. "Same."

"Nice to know." He laid his hand on her thigh.

Her womb clenched in response, making her gasp.

"Too much?" His murmured question ramped up the heat flooding her body. He glanced at her, eyebrows lifted.

The warmth of his hand drove her crazy, but she didn't want him to move it. Gulping, she shook her head. It would be a very long evening.

_15_

Riding back to town with his hand on Jordan's thigh thrilled Luis more than a stunning laser show that had cost the town thousands. He'd exclaimed over the display right along with the rest of his family. Meanwhile he'd ached for another chance to touch Jordan.

But she wasn't within reach. To keep his family from picking up on the sparks flying between them, he'd deliberately avoided sitting next to her for the show. Easy to do. She'd been swept into the Hearts & Hooves group the moment they'd returned.

The laser show finale couldn't come soon enough for him. But he still didn't seek her out as the huge crowd migrated to the Raccoon. How many dances could he claim before everyone in town figured things out?

None. But he wanted, _needed_ to dance with her. If this weekend would have to last him a lifetime, he wanted dancing to be part of the memory. And not a fast two-step. A waltz.

As he blended in with the slow-moving crowd, Monty caught up with him. "Mila and Claudie asked me to give you the word."

"What's that?"

Monty glanced around as if checking for eavesdroppers. Then he lowered his voice. "They'd like the three of us to invite the H&H women to dance. I agree it would be a nice gesture."

"You, me and Zay?"

"Right. Rio's excused since he has a date."

"I can help out."

"What about Jordan?"

"You want her to dance with the ladies, too?"

"You know what I mean. You've been avoiding her ever since we got back to town. Are you okay dancing with her?"

"Sure. But just once."

"Ouch. That's cold, bro."

He chuckled. "You think we had a fight?"

"Looks like it from the cheap seats."

"We didn't have a fight. I just don't want to be... obvious."

"Ahh. Mission accomplished. We all think you're on the outs."

"Not."

"Happy to hear it. This plan should help your cause. With the three of us switching around, nobody will think anything about you dancing with her."

"That's how I want it."

"I'm really glad you didn't have a fight. After the cozy connection you two had as we rode into town, I assumed you'd decided—"

"You were supposed to be asleep."

"I was playing possum to give you lovebirds some privacy. I'd intended to sleep, but quickly realized I'd better stay alert. I didn't fancy ending up in a ditch."

"Don't be ridiculous. I wasn't—"

"Oh, no? Every time I checked, either she was staring at you or you were staring at her. Or you were staring at each other and the only one watching the road was yours truly."

"For a split second, okay?"

Monty grinned. "I'm just messing with you, bro. Mostly I'm jealous. No woman's looked at me that way in months."

"Because you don't give them a chance." They were still several yards from the Raccoon's front door, which was propped open to allow the noisy crowd to funnel through it. "You're working all the damn time."

"Pot, meet kettle."

"It's not my fault. I'm trying to find an assistant but nobody's right for it."

"Because they're not Dad?"

He sighed. "Yeah." Lively country music poured into the street and many outside were already dancing. "It would be great if it could be someone from the family, but Greta wants to be a chef, Zay's got a future as an artist, whether he knows it or not. And Rio...."

"I know. Lacks focus. I wish Jordan—"

"Not happening."

"Now that I've seen her rig, I get it. She's invested in her business. She's not giving it up to work for us."

"I wouldn't want her to. She loves it."

Monty clapped him on the shoulder. "Sorry for your sake. I can tell that you... well, never mind."

"I can handle it."

"I know you can." Monty held his gaze for a moment, his unspoken message clear. He'd be there when the shit hit the fan. No one in the Bridger Bunch suffered alone.

Then he turned toward the Raccoon. "Hey, look at that. We're almost through the door. Now the challenge is scoring a couple of beers."

"Not your problem, *hermano*. I'm buying." He and Monty plunged into the red, white and blue chaos. An explosion of bunting, streamers, balloons and colored lights continued the celebration's patriotic vibe.

Clem pulled out all the stops twice a year — New Year's Eve and Independence Day. Since musicians needed a break between sets, he'd hired a back-up band so the music never stopped.

Technically Clem had three bands, counting the Rockin' Raccoons. He always made time to show off his animatronic musical trio mounted on a platform over the bar. Tonight they wore Uncle Sam top hats and white whiskers. Where Clem found embellishments like that was a mystery.

The raccoon trio was silent and unmoving now, but periodically during the night Clem would signal the band to pause before playing the next tune. Then he'd get on the mic, bellow *Give it up for the Raccoooons* and flip a switch.

Those little critters would take it from there, plucking the bass strings, playing the fiddle and pounding on the ivories. The Rockin' Raccoon theme song always brought folks to their feet to clap and sing along.

Luis cherished every bit of it. That didn't mean he wanted to stay a minute more than was necessary. Any other year he'd be among the last to leave. Now he wouldn't mind being the first.

But he had to play it cool. He'd promised Monty a beer, and the crowd at the bar was four deep.

He glanced at his brother. "Wanna see if the Bunch has a table staked out?"

"Will do." He split off, heading left into the packed dining area.

Luis turned toward the bar and came face-to-face with Jordan holding a mug of beer in each hand.

She looked as startled as he was. "Hey!" Her cheeks turned pink.

"Hey, yourself. Where's your H&H hat?" Was that the best he could do? Comment on her lack of headgear?

"I left it at the table. My head was getting hot."

"Oh." He'd apply that description to all of her. Even dressed in a loose-fitting T-shirt and jeans, she was the sexiest woman he'd ever come across.

"I was wondering if I'd see you at all tonight. It's been crazy."

"Always is." He couldn't stop looking into those sparkling blue eyes. They were telegraphing all the things. Arousing his body and hijacking his brain. "I... um... save me a dance, okay?"

She smiled. "How am I supposed to do that?"

"I have no idea. It's something guys say. I guess we're trying to find out if you'll say yes when we ask you or shut us down."

"I'll say yes." She lifted the mugs. "I should probably—"

"Oh! Yeah, sorry." He'd blocked her forward progress. Stepping aside, he tipped his hat. "Didn't mean to keep you from delivering those."

"One's for Monty. I haven't found him yet. Have you?"

"We came in together. He just went to see if the Bunch has grabbed a table."

"They did. Sort of. A couple of tables and some wall space for leaning against. I'll just work my way back over there."

"Where are they?"

"Far corner on the street side."

"Got it. How about the women who came for the H&H tour?"

"We're there, too. Get yourself a beer and come join us."

"I will. See you soon." He resisted the impulse to follow her and forget about the beer. No point in buying one for Monty now, and being in her orbit would give him more of a buzz than any brand of alcohol.

But hustling over there without a beer would be the exact opposite of playing it cool. For the time being, he'd have to be on guard against knee-jerk reactions.

Such as standing here like an idiot watching her thread her way through the crowded room while keeping those beers from spilling. That took concentration and a keen sense of spatial awareness. She'd demonstrated both abilities on day one of the clinic they'd attended.

Working effectively with uncooperative or frightened horses required a unique set of talents. Jordan had them all. She was likely even better at it, now.

So was he. When it came to understanding the magnificent animals they both loved, the learning process never stopped.

Forcing himself to move in the opposite direction, he claimed a spot in the ever-shifting mass of humanity in front of the antique bar. The band finished two numbers and was launching into a third before he finally had a foam-topped mug in hand.

Now to make it over to the far corner of the room. The Bridger Bunch took up space. The immediate family, including the aunties and Grandma Doris numbered fourteen, because now they officially counted Adam's wife Tracy and her folks Jeff and Carrie.

Mila and Claudie had added the women from the tour group to the mix, making it more than twenty. As he approached, he eyed the situation. Looked like he'd be leaning against the wall like his brothers while he sipped his beer.

"There's my dance partner!" Auntie Kat popped out of her seat. "I adore this song, Luis. Will you please ask me to dance?"

He laughed and found a spot on one of the tables for his beer. "Auntie Kat, will you give me the honor of a dance?"

"I'd love to, dear boy." She tucked her arm through his. "I'll count on you to clear the way. What a mob. I think it's worse than last year."

"Or better. Don't forget Clem's donating a portion of the take to H&H."

"I did forget. Thanks for reminding me."

He led her out on the dance floor. "Do you really like this song? It doesn't sound like you."

"I think it's dopey, but I had a brainstorm and couldn't wait to tell you. Since it's a slow two-step we can talk and dance at the same time."

"You don't want to wait until tomorrow to tell me? It can't be that urgent." He twirled her around the floor.

"It might be." She matched his steps perfectly. "It's about your assistant."

He sucked in a breath. "Tell me you're not suggesting Jordan."

"I'm not. I promised her I wouldn't interfere with whatever is going on with you two. Never mind that you're perfect for each other."

"Except for one unsolvable problem."

"Nothing's unsolvable. You're just not thinking outside the box. And don't roll your eyes at me, Luis Bridger."

"*Perdon*, Auntie." Thinking outside the box was one of her favorite lines and they'd all heard it a million times. "What about my assistant? If you want the job, it's yours."

"I wouldn't be half bad but I have someone else in mind." She executed a tricky step, twirled under his arm and was facing him again. "Rio."

"Rio? You're kidding."

"I'm dead serious."

"But he's never shown the slightest—"

"He doesn't think he's good enough."

"He told you that?"

"No, but I have eyes and ears, and since he's living in my house now, I have an excuse to drop in and chat with him."

"About him becoming my assistant?"

"Of course not! I would never suggest that to him." She spun under his arm again. "But I'd be thrilled if you'd do it. That boy's lost. He's searching for a purpose."

"That's why he's wrong for the job. He lacks focus."

"Give him a reason to focus. He worships you."

"Auntie, I love you to pieces, but if Rio had any interest in working with wild horses he would've shown it by now."

"He's out there all the time monitoring the water tanks and checking the electric fence line."

"But he's never asked to go with me. I started following Dad around when I was a kid."

"And by high school you and Spence were a team. A tight team. No room for little Rio."

He felt that one deep in his chest where truth usually landed.

Her voice softened. "I see something in him, Luis. You could do for him what Spence did for you."

Another direct hit, this time to the knot of grief that hadn't loosened yet. Maybe never would. "I'll talk with him."

The dance ended. Perfect timing, one of Auntie Kat's superpowers. Standing on tiptoe, she kissed him on the cheek. "Thank you."

<u>16</u>

As the night wore on and Luis danced with all the H&H women except her, Jordan began to wonder what his *save a dance for me* comment had been about. She'd been out on the floor quite a bit, too, but he'd still had plenty of opportunity to ask her.

The emotional rollercoaster reminded her of dances in middle school when the girls had been eager and the boys had been shy. Not that Luis was shy. He looked like a man having a great time.

He was also damn good at this. So was she, if she did say so. They could be tearing up that floor. Should she ask him, instead? Like Kat had?

No. She'd done enough by coming here in the first place. This was his town, his family. He needed to make the call.

But in the meantime, she could show off a little, just in case he was keeping tabs on her, too. She put enough energy into every fast two-step to keep the fringe on her boots in constant shimmy mode. Still no invitation from Luis.

Eventually the crowd started to thin out. She caught Mila covering a yawn. When Adam announced he'd go settle the bill, the prospect of dancing with Luis grew dim. The Bridger Bunch would probably leave after this next number.

It turned out to be an old Alan Jackson song called *You've Got Me Right Where I Want You.* For sure he wouldn't ask her when the tune was slow and romantic. She located her backpack and swallowed her disappointment.

Then he appeared, smiling as he held out his hand. "Dance with me?"

She jumped up so fast her chair would have hit the floor if he hadn't caught it. He steadied it with his free hand and then led her out on the floor. "Sorry about being so late."

"No worries." Although she was a little worried and a lot shaky. Only a few couples were dancing. Sort of. More like snuggling. Was that what he had in mind?

She sent him a questioning glance. Holding her gaze, he placed a firm hand in the middle of her back and raised their clasped hands to shoulder height. "Let's waltz." He whirled her onto the floor.

Her heart stuttered, then settled into the gentle *one*-two-three, *one*-two-three beat of the song. "Did you request this?"

"Yes, ma'am."

"Why?"

"Figured you wouldn't be expecting it."

"That's for sure."

"And there's less body contact. Safer that way."

"Doesn't feel safe." The intensity in his deep brown eyes held her captive as the graceful symmetry of the dance echoed the rhythm of making slow, sweet, love. Memorable love, like their last time on that golden morning. "It's sneaky seductive."

"I know." He smiled. "I wanted to improve my odds."

"Ever hear of overkill?"

His smile widened. "Really?"

"Uh-huh."

"Good." He let out a sigh. "Thought you might have changed your—"

"Nope." Between the dance and her racing heart, she was low on air. "I can't wait."

His eyes darkened. "Wanna make a break for it?"

"Don't tempt me."

"Too late." He dragged in a breath. "Damn, Jordan."

"Damn, Luis."

"You turned the tables on me, lady. I'm in the palm of your hand. Tell me what we should do."

"I can't ride back with you."

"You could, but you'd have to sit on Monty's lap."

That startled a laugh out of her. "Which would kinda blow our cover."

"If we still have any. I'd hoped to do this early in the evening. We're a bit conspicuous."

"Are they all watching us?"

He glanced toward the corner of the room. "Yep."

"This is silly. I should tell your mom I'll be staying with you."

His eyes widened. "You'd do that?"

"Now that I know her better, I'm guessing she'd appreciate honesty instead of sneaking around. It's more respectful."

His chest heaved. "Alrighty, then. Full disclosure?"

"Full disclosure."

"Song's almost over."

"I loved this waltz."

"Me, too." He twirled her around once more and ended with a dramatic dip that brought a round of applause from their audience. Then his lips brushed hers, just a whisper of a kiss.

The applause grew louder with a few whistles thrown in. Being open was the way to go.

Scared her, though. She had butterflies when Luis ushered her back to the table. Her cheeks warmed and she had to clear her throat. "Raquel, thank you for offering me one of your guest rooms, but—"

"You'll be staying with Luis." She looked both amused and curious as hell. "We figured that out. Rio's going home with us in the van and Adam's taking Zay and Monty. You two can leave whenever you want."

"Oh! Well, um…"

"*Gracias, Mama.*" Luis leaned over and kissed her cheek.

"Your backpack, Jordan." Mila handed it over with a wink. "Don't forget the book signing."

She gasped. "I absolutely won't! I—"

"She's teasing you," Claudie said, laughing. "Get outta here, both of you, before you combust."

"We're off." Luis grabbed his hat and took her hand.

"Wait." She pulled him to a halt. "Monty, how was Fudge on your last check?"

"He looked fine. I'll pay him a visit when we get back."

"Thank you. So will I." She turned toward Luis. "Now we can go."

With a quick nod, he led the way through the mostly deserted dining area.

"That was some hot dancing, *hermano*," Rio called after them. "You need to teach me that."

Luis raised a hand in acknowledgement as he ushered her out the door. Weaving his fingers through hers, he let out a breath as they headed down the sidewalk lined with old-fashioned lamp posts.

"Where'd you learn to waltz?"

"Mom and Dad loved it. Where did you?"

"When I shared an apartment with Cole. We'd picked up whatever dancing skills we had at country bars, but then he got the urge to learn the classics so we took lessons."

"Your voice changes when you talk about him."

"Like how?"

"Softer, warmer. You really care about your brother."

"Yeah, and I need to pay him a visit. Last time we talked on the phone he made me promise it would be soon."

"Where is he?"

"Helena. I considered asking if he wanted to come here for the weekend. I'm sure he's off work, but...."

"You didn't want him to meet me."

"Not just that. He likes the M.R. Morrison books but I don't know if he'd be into a book signing. He'd probably be interested in H&H, but would he want a tour? I can't say."

"You haven't told him about it?"

"No." She glanced at him. "Okay, you're right. I've avoided telling him about H&H because you're involved. If he'd come this weekend... it's already complicated enough without adding Cole to the mix."

"Since my presence is such an issue, I'm amazed *you* came."

"Like I said, I thought you'd be married by now. That would've solved everything."

"Explain that to me again."

"I'd see you with the love of your life and maybe even a couple of adorable kids. You'd be doing exactly what you should be doing and I—" She stopped herself but likely not soon enough.

"And what?"

"You get the gist."

"If I would just play my expected role you could forget about me?"

Evidently honesty was her default setting tonight. "Yes."

"Sorry to disappoint you." He pulled out his keys. "Given what you just said, I should withdraw my invitation."

She gulped. "Please don't."

"I'm not that noble. But what I have in mind isn't going to help your cause."

17

Jordan's quick intake of breath and the subtle quiver of her body as Luis handed her into his truck was exactly what he was going for. Hearing that she desperately wanted to forget him pricked his ego. He wanted to make sure she never did.

He wasn't proud of that, but he might as well not kid himself. His intentions weren't entirely honorable.

Comments like he'd just made were a double-edged sword, though. His blood ran hot as he rounded the truck and climbed into the cab.

Satisfaction was a thirty-minute drive away and they had to check on Fudge before they could get busy. His jeans pinched. Time to cool his jets.

He started the engine and switched off the music. "How'd you like the laser show?"

"Loved it. Fireworks are beautiful, but I've always hated the noise, even before I found out how it terrifies animals. Points to Mustang Valley for switching."

"It was Dad's idea. He lobbied hard for it."

"After seeing the ranch today, I'm not surprised. Wish I'd met him."

"Too bad I stood in the way of that."

"That's my fault, not yours. If I'd been braver…."

"Or if I hadn't made a move on you in the first place." As he drove away from town, he glanced in the rearview to check for lights from either the van or Adam's truck. *Nada.*

"You think you started it?"

"Sure. I'm the one who knocked on your motel room door and asked you to dinner." The road behind him remained empty. They were giving him a nice long head start.

"If you hadn't, I would have knocked on yours. I wanted to continue the conversation we'd had at the end of the afternoon session. Things were just getting interesting."

"So we would have had dinner one way or the other?"

"Yep. And once we found out we were both unattached…."

He chuckled. "I spent the rest of that meal trying to remember if we'd passed a convenience store on the way to the diner."

"You were so cute, pretending you were going in for cigarettes. I couldn't believe you were a smoker."

He grimaced. "Only excuse I could come up with. I still didn't know for sure that you—"

"You didn't know? After all my outrageous flirting?"

"I could see you liked me, but we'd known each other for like seven or eight hours, tops. I've never moved that fast with anyone else. That's not me."

"But we didn't have weeks to get acquainted. Just looking at you across that chipped Formica tabletop did it for me. I thought about condoms, too, and wondered if you traveled with them."

"And you'd have been fine with that?"

"I wasn't in a mood to judge whether you did this all the time or not. Then you had to stop and buy a box, which charmed the pants off me. Literally."

He remembered those jeans, faded from many washings, supple and easy to deal with.... And here he was fixated on the subject he'd told himself to avoid, at least until they were closer to home.

He looked in the side mirror. Still no headlights, but he caught a glimpse of his beard. "I'd planned to shave before you came over."

"Don't worry about it."

"But—"

"You had scruff that first night, too. I found it sexy."

"I was younger. It was softer then. I don't want to scratch you."

"If you're worried, you can shave while I go down to see Fudge."

"I want to check on him, too." He also wasn't letting her out of his sight. He had no reason to think she'd change her mind at the last minute, but he wasn't taking any chances. "I'll just be careful how I kiss you."

"I wonder if you taste the same."

He groaned. "Let's not talk about—"

"You're the one who brought up kissing."

A quick glance confirmed that she was smiling. "Are you deliberately—"

"You bet I am." She lowered her voice. "*What I have in mind won't help your cause.* You know damn well what that did to me. I'm gunning for you, cowboy."

And didn't that just send a jolt of lust straight to his privates? "Fair enough."

"And when we finally get inside your cozy casita, we're going from zero to sixty. No side trips, no fancy foreplay."

"Got it." Had he left lights on? He didn't want to stumble around in the— *yikes, the turnoff.* He squeaked the tires as he wrenched the wheel to the right and swerved onto the ranch road.

"I wondered if you'd drive right past it."

"Having fun?"

"I am. I haven't had this much fun since...." Her voice trailed off.

"Five years ago?"

"You guessed it."

He swallowed the words he wanted to say, the vision he longed to share — her clinic based here, their lives and skills woven together for the sake of the majestic animals they loved.

Pulling over to the keypad post, he put down his window and listened.

"Checking for horses?"

"It's a habit. If any were lingering around the gate, I likely scared them off with my squealing tires." He tapped in the code and the large gate swung open.

"It must be a thrill, surrounded by herds of wild horses all the time."

"I love it." He drove through and looked over his shoulder to make sure the gate closed. "And so do they, once they understand that food and water are always available and they're free to run. Eventually they realize nobody's gonna shoot at 'em."

"To think it's been going for twenty years."

"Yes, ma'am." He flicked on his brights and kept his attention on the road in case any critters decided to cross in front of him.

"You must have been so excited when your folks made the decision."

"It was huge, especially for those of us who were old enough to see how cool it was. Monty sort of got it, but Rio and Greta, not so much. They can't remember a time when H&H didn't exist."

"I remember you telling me the ranch had a sanctuary, but I didn't appreciate the scope. I imagined a few horses in a pasture, not hundreds living on thousands of acres."

"My family tends to think big." He treasured that. Pulling over, he keyed in the code to open the gate into the ranch compound.

"Speaking of your family, where are they? I thought they were ready to leave, too, but we seem to be all alone out here."

"I'm pretty sure that's on purpose. They're giving us time to get settled in my casita." Which wouldn't be long now. The buzz of anticipation made him a little shaky as he drove the short distance to his house.

"Good grief. I had no idea they'd hang back."

"When you live this close together, you learn how to give each other space." Now he really had the shakes. Parking next to his casita, he shut off the engine and hopped out. Almost stumbled.

By the time he made it around the tailgate to the passenger door, she'd climbed out. The soft glow from the hanging lanterns on his patio touched her hair, her cheeks, the gentle rise and fall of her breasts.

He'd never make it to the barn and back without hauling her into his arms. "Maybe you should go see Fudge on your own."

"So you can shave?"

"Right." He'd give it a try, although he might slice himself to ribbons.

"Okay." Her little smile said she was onto him. "I guess it would be embarrassing to get caught making out in the barn."

"That, too."

"Can you take my backpack?"

"Sure thing."

She came toward him and handed it over.

The light brush of her fingers against his was nearly his undoing. He tightened his jaw.

"See you in a few minutes." She gave him a quick glance. "Careful with that razor."

As she walked away, he dragged in a breath. He was in over his head, might even drown. But there was no turning back.

_18_

Jordan quickened her step, eager for a chance to catch her breath and rein in her turbulent emotions. When she'd agreed to this, she hadn't factored in the seductive nature of the environment.

Five years ago Luis had transformed a nondescript motel room into paradise. What effect would he have when they actually _were_ in paradise?

Laughing Creek had captured her heart the moment she'd driven through its front gate this afternoon. By establishing a sanctuary for hundreds of horses with their large family smack dab in the middle of it, the Bridger Bunch had created something magical.

And she would soon make love to a key player in sustaining that magic, the sanctuary's resident horse whisperer. Might as well admit the experience would be epic.

Thank goodness she'd set her boundaries and had a schedule to maintain. When they'd met that hadn't been the case, but she'd still managed to hold onto her plan for the future.

A breeze touched her hot skin, bringing with it the tangy scent of crushed grass. Snorts and the soft thud of hooves from the nearby pasture blended with the chirp of crickets.

A half-moon and a handful of stars decorated the cloudless sky. Lights twinkling from the homes on the property gave her the feeling of being surrounded by a friendly village.

She headed for the barn where Fudge was stabled. A smaller barn partially hidden behind it was used for wild horses Luis brought in to train so they'd be adoptable. Mila had said it was empty for now.

Too bad. She would have liked to watch him work with those horses. But he'd temporarily paused that part of the operation in advance of the holiday because it was labor intensive.

Stepping though the open door into the barn, she stopped to let her eyes adjust. Small lights spaced along the aisle helped guide her over to Fudge's stall.

Slowly she unlatched the door and stepped in. He was lying down, but in a different part of the stall, so he'd been up, probably to finish off his oats and hay. The bucket and hay net were both empty.

He lifted his head and softly knickered.

"Hey, Fudgie." She knelt down and took his head in her lap. "How're you doing?"

In response he made the little noise in his throat that was his signature reply whenever her voice rose in a question.

She let out a breath, relieved and grateful. "Glad to hear you're feeling better." He wouldn't make that noise if he was hurting.

Combing her fingers through his forelock, she rubbed his nose and stroked his neck. "It's been quite a day. You with your hoof and me trying to decide—" She caught herself and changed course. "Whether I should accept the Bridgers' hospitality or not."

Normally she confessed all her secrets to Fudge. Did Monty's camera record audio? Better to assume it did and watch what she said. "As you can guess, I decided to accept it."

Fudge's head became heavier as he relaxed against her. "Time for you to get some more sleep." When she started to move away he lifted his head again. "Monty will be here soon to check on you." She gave him a kiss on his nose. "I'll be back to see you in the morning. Sleep tight, sweet boy."

He kept watching her as she backed out of the stall. Blowing him another kiss, she closed and latched the door. The straw rustled as he settled down again.

She walked out of the barn a much calmer person. Her pal Fudge was on the mend and they both knew it. The special bond they shared had a soothing effect on each of them.

Breathing in a lungful of cool air, she let it out slowly, centering herself. Tonight she would enjoy hot sex with a wonderful man. And she would keep it in perspective.

That mindset served her well until she reached the casita's low patio wall and stepped through the open gate. Luis rose from one of the patio chairs, his broad-shouldered silhouette filling her with a desperate hunger that incinerated every rational thought in her head.

"*Bienvenida, querida.*"

With a low moan, she hurled herself into his arms.

He caught her and laughed in delight as he swept her up and carried her through the open door. He kicked it shut. "How's Fudge?"

She gulped for air. "He's good." Arms around his neck, cradled against his muscular chest, she drank in the sight of his strong profile and the endearing dent in his smooth cheek. "Did you cut yourself?"

"No, ma'am."

"Well done." She should be noticing the house he was taking her through, but she was having a moment. No man had ever carried her to bed, not even him.

Then he stepped into his bedroom and she couldn't help but notice her surroundings. Flickering votives were everywhere. "Oh, my." Her heart melted. He'd remembered.

"Like it?"

"You know I do." So did he. Before their second night together they'd combed the small mountain town for votives and come up empty. "But the shops were all closed today."

"The owner of the General Store's a friend of mine. Fetched me a big box of them this afternoon." He slowly lowered her to her feet. "And now I'm going to kiss you properly."

She slid her arms around him and looked up into those incredible eyes. Her body clamored for his kiss, his touch, all of him loving all of her. "Yes, please."

Cupping her face in his warm hands, he leaned down. "Let me know if I taste the same." Then he settled those smiling lips against hers... and instantly swept her back five years to that motel room.

Shivering in reaction, she held on tight as he made slow, sweet love to her mouth. Her nipples tightened and her panties dampened.

This was his superpower. He could almost make her come just by kissing her. And he tasted delicious.

Putting a fraction of an inch between his lips and hers, he gulped for air. "I love kissing you. I don't want to stop."

"Just let go for one sec." She stepped away, fumbled for the hem of her T-shirt, and yanked it over her head. Then she lifted her face and closed her eyes. "Carry on."

With a groan, he shoved his fingers through her hair and recaptured her mouth. She grabbed hold of his shirt and started on the buttons but excitement made her clumsy.

His jeans would be easier. As she undid the metal button and tugged on the zipper, he backed her toward the bed until her legs hit the mattress.

He ended the kiss with a soft groan of frustration. "Clothes. We need to—"

"You get yours. I'll get mine." That was what they'd done before. It was faster.

Within seconds they'd ditched their clothes and tumbled onto the bed where he continued her favorite pastime. Only now he didn't confine himself to her mouth.

The dancing flames of the votives kept time with her wildly beating heart as he covered her with kisses. Every touch of his warm mouth ramped up the tension until she was writhing beneath him.

She gasped out a plea. "We said... no... foreplay."

"I'm not playing, *querida*." His soft words tickled the damp skin of her inner thighs. "I'm serious." And he claimed her with an intimate kiss that sent her into the stratosphere.

Her world spun around her, a carousel of light and shadow laced with intense pleasure. No one could blur the lines between reality and fantasy the way he could. In his arms she became lighter than air and bubbling over with joy.

She was vaguely aware of the mattress shifting and a familiar crinkling sound. Her body, still quivering in the aftermath of a spectacular release, responded with a fresh surge of longing.

When the mattress dipped again, the heat of his body and the brush of his thighs against hers created a deep ache that made her whimper. When he murmured her name, she opened her eyes.

Braced on his forearms, he gazed down at her, his breathing fast, his eyes dark. But a frown creased his brow and his voice was soft, almost tender. "That little sound you made... if you're not ready, I can wait."

She swallowed. "I want you so much I can't stand it."

The frown disappeared and he let out a breath. "*Gracias Dios.* I thought you—"

She wrapped him in her arms. "Love me. Right now."

He complied. Holy smokes did that cowboy comply!

She'd been without this activity for a while, but even so. He had rhythm. He had skill. And he had the goods to deliver... almost more than she could handle.

Deep penetration and irresistible friction soon had her panting and calling his name. Then the storm broke a second time, hurling her into a timeless world filled with endless waves of bliss.

Cupping her tush in his big hands, he held her fast as he continued to pump, his gaze locked with hers. "Again."

His voice, thick with passion, stirred a response in her core. As she tightened around his cock, he picked up the pace, his breathing ragged, his grip insistent. The headboard smacked against the wall, again and again and again.

With a wild cry she erupted, arching into each rapid thrust. Shouting in triumph, he drove deep and let go. His powerful contractions blended with hers as he closed his eyes and bowed his head.

She sank back to the mattress, sweaty and dazed. She'd never made love like this. Not even with him. And the perspective she'd vowed to keep? Gone.

<u>19</u>

Dios mio. Luis sucked in a breath as his sanity slowly returned. Had it been this incredible the last time he'd made love with Jordan? No. Wonderful, yes. But he hadn't come apart like a pinata, gasping and dizzy, twirling and disoriented.

Lifting his head, he gazed down into blue eyes filled with the same shock and uncertainty gripping him. He swallowed. "You okay?"

She shook her head.

"Me, neither." Leaning down, he kissed her gently before easing away from the warm cradle of her body. He didn't want to go. Breaking their intimate connection took an effort of will. "We'll talk." He headed for his bathroom.

"Okay." She sounded hoarse. Probably from all that yelling.

He'd figured they would make noise and had closed the windows before going to wait for her on the patio. He'd given himself a little pep talk, too, promising to keep the end game in mind. She would leave. He'd accepted that.

The hell he had. He could say it all he wanted, but his body had other ideas. His ego, too.

From the moment she'd thrown herself into his arms, basic instincts had taken over.

They were still driving the bus. As he washed up, his cock twitched, wanting more. What was it about this woman? Was it because she was out of reach?

If so, that was jacked up. In any event, he'd seriously miscalculated how intense this interlude could be. He needed to bail. Now.

Returning to the bedroom, he was treated to a familiar sight — Jordan propped against the headboard, a pillow behind her back. The sheets were still tangled at the foot of the bed.

During their previous nights together, they'd made love and then sat in bed talking. They'd discussed anything and everything until a glance or a subtle nudge had them rolling around on the mattress again.

Votives hadn't been part of the mix, though. The flames bathed her creamy skin in a golden glow, just as he'd imagined they would.

He'd always loved gazing at her body, but the votives made the experience more erotic. His fingers curled with the need to caress her warm, satin-smooth curves. Could he blame candlelight for hijacking his brain?

Doubtful. After the enthusiastic welcome she'd given his cock, he'd been oblivious to his surroundings. The whole damn house could've caught fire and he would have kept on loving her with all that was in him.

"I can tell you're thinking. Care to tell me what's on your mind?"

"You, *querida.*" He approached the bed. "Just you." If he got back in, he'd make love to her again. He should deliver his speech from here.

"Then we're even, because I've been thinking about you." She patted the spot next to her. "Come sit. We'll compare notes."

The comment touched his heart. During their previous encounters that had meant comparing notes on the day's training session.

Horse-related pillow talk. Only Jordan would think that was fun, and he'd loved that about her.

He might as well face it. He wasn't going to deliver that speech. Not now, anyway.

He climbed in beside her. "I don't have any notes. My brain checked out during that episode. If you have some pointers that would improve my technique, go for it."

"That isn't what I meant."

"I know." Shoving a pillow behind his back, he reached for her hand and wove his fingers through hers. Their previous conversations in bed had included holding hands. "I'm being a smartass because I have no freaking idea what to say."

"Me, either, except... that was the best damn sex I've ever had."

His fingers tightened. "Same."

"Oh, dear." She turned her head to look at him. "That's bad news."

"Tell me about it." He held her gaze. "Kinda messes up the concept of a frisky romp in the hay with no consequences."

"But we managed before."

"We did." He kept his focus on her eyes. Letting his attention wander would end the discussion and maybe a solution would come out if they talked things through.

"Are we just better at this now?"

He nodded. "Could be. We're older. More experienced."

"If that's the reason, we'd have had great sex with other people."

"True." Dealing with this topic while naked presented quite the challenge. "To be perfectly honest, five years ago was the best I'd ever had. Until now."

"I wasn't planning to admit that."

He shifted, turning more in her direction. "We need to be straight with each other."

Her gaze flickered.

He squeezed her hand. "We were last time. We didn't pull any punches."

"You're right." She took a deep breath. "If I'm honest with myself, I adopted the H&H horses because it created a connection to you."

His heartbeat ramped up a notch. "I wondered about that."

"I liked being a tiny part of the project you care so much about. But then...." She looked away. "I had this dream about you."

"Only one? I've had dozens about you. Mostly X-rated."

"I've had those, too, but this was different. You asked me to come to you. You said we... we belong together."

His brain stalled. "That's what brought you here? To find out if we—"

"Good heavens, no. Clearly we *don't* belong together. We both know that."

She might know it. He was no longer sure.

"That stupid dream stuck with me just like the earworm of a song you can't get rid of. If you had been married, that would likely have squashed it. I searched for clues on the website. Couldn't find any."

"Nothing to find." And why was he still single? Another good question. Was he a one-woman man? That would suck.

"I was still convinced you had to be married or at least engaged. Since I couldn't confirm it online, I had a perfect excuse to come see for myself."

"What was your Plan B?"

"Didn't have one."

"That's not like you."

"In my mind, odds of you being available were ninety-nine to one." She turned back to him. "At the very least you'd have a serious girlfriend. That wouldn't be as solid, but if you were in love with someone, better yet if I saw you with her acting all lovey-dovey, I'd be free of that blasted dream."

"Will you tell me about it?"

"Why?"

"Just curious. Maybe there's something in there that would help dismantle it."

"Okay." She settled back against the pillow. "It was twilight, my favorite time of day."

"Night. It's not day anymore at twilight."

"Yes, it is. There's still light in the sky from the sun, which makes it part of the day."

"The percentage of dark is more than the percentage of light, which makes it part of the night. The evening star comes out. They don't call it the daylight star."

"Do you really want to argue about this?"

"I kinda do. Reminds me of the debates we used to have, like whether Scout is more of a Paint than a pinto."

"Paint."

"Pinto."

"We can forget about the dream. I don't think you really—"

"No, no, I want to hear about it. And FYI, twilight is my favorite time, too." Especially after the clinic experience. Twilight meant he could be alone with her.

"Okay, then. I was in this grassy field at twilight for some reason. Then a horse and rider came toward me at a gallop."

"Me, I assume."

"Right. Even at a distance I could tell it was you. You have a distinctive style."

"I do?"

"Great posture, excellent form, but there's nothing stiff about you."

He chuckled. "Don't be so sure. After all, I was coming to see you."

She gave him a look.

"Sorry. Carry on."

"You rode up on Scout, a beautiful butterscotch Paint—"

"Pinto."

"You swung down from the saddle and dropped the reins. When you walked toward me, I thought you were going to kiss me. You had that gleam in your eyes."

"Like now?"

She smiled. "Like now."

"Then what?"

"Using your low sexy voice, you said *Come to me, querida. We belong together.*"

"Did I kiss you?"

"No. You faded away and I woke up."

"Hmm. I didn't kiss you, we didn't make love, and you've rejected the idea that we belong together. I don't understand what's so compelling about this dream."

"I don't, either! But I keep seeing the intensity in your eyes and hearing the urgency in your voice."

"Just at night?"

"Mostly. Or at twilight."

"How about since we reconnected this morning?"

"I've been too involved with the real you to have your dream self popping in for a visit."

"I have a theory. Burning up the sheets might have wiped out that image for good."

"Maybe. I can see how it could. But I'm afraid it's created...." She trailed off, as if reluctant to put her fears into words.

"A bigger problem?"

She nodded.

"I won't lie. It already has. When I left the bathroom I'd planned to call a halt to save myself. And save you, for that matter."

Her breath caught.

"Couldn't do it."

"It's hard when we're in bed naked."

He grinned.

"Oh, for pity's sake! I'm trying to be serious."

"Let's not be. Just for tonight."

"And then?"

"We'll be serious tomorrow. We'll evaluate. We'll make smart choices."

She snuggled closer. "Are you saying this is dumb?"

"Yes, ma'am. Completely stupid." He slid down and patted his chest. "Wanna come over here, pretty lady?"

"Sure." She settled on top of him and nestled her cheek in the curve of his neck.

Felt so damn good lying beneath her warm body. Stroking her back, he let out a deep sigh. "We're a couple of idiots."

"Uh-huh."

He combed his fingers through her hair. "Will you make love to this crazy moron, *querida*?"

"With pleasure." Lifting her head, she gave him a sizzling kiss. He was immediately hard as the tailpipe on his truck.

Reaching for a condom on the nightstand, she sat back and tore open the foil wrapper. He tucked a pillow under his head so he could watch. Being suited up by Jordan was his favorite way to accomplish the task.

Her little frown of concentration was adorable, and dealing with his cock turned her on as much as it did him. She was efficient about it, too, which aroused him even more.

He propped his hands behind his head so he wouldn't reach for her and try to direct the action. Her independent spirit craved control and he gladly gave it to her.

By the time she finished and was straddling him, he had to clench his jaw so he wouldn't come in the first few seconds.

She needed eye contact during sex just like he did. Holding his gaze, her palms flat on his chest, she lowered her sweet tush, taking him in up to the hilt. "How's that?"

He pretended nonchalance. It was a game they'd played. "Passable."

Her low, sexy laughter fit with the heat in her eyes. "I'm coming for you, cowboy."

"Please do." He was the luckiest cuss in the world, lying here being loved by this amazing woman. The reckoning would come soon enough. But not yet.

20

Jordan cherished the way Luis encouraged her to take charge. He'd done it from their first night together. They'd met as equals in the training arena and continued as equals in bed.

His dark eyes glittered as she began to pump.

"Good?"

"Yes, ma'am."

Her body reacted to his husky reply by clenching the muscles surrounding his cock.

His eyes widened and he sucked in a breath.

"On edge, are you?" She picked up speed.

He spoke through gritted teeth. "You could say that."

"Want to hold onto me?"

"Yes." His eyes darkened. "Yes, I do." Abandoning his semi-relaxed pose, he cupped her ass.

He could have used his grip to control the pace. Instinctively she knew he wouldn't. Her choice, her show.

He had the self-control to keep it that way. No wonder sex with him was the best ever.

Her climax drew near, stealing her breath, stealing her sanity. She moved faster, craving that sweet release.

He groaned, but didn't tighten his hold or try to slow her down. She got the message, though. He didn't want to come yet. But she was past the point of no return.

"Don't... worry," she gasped out. "We'll do this... again."

He clenched his jaw. "Promise?"

"Cross my heart." And she went for it, riding him for all she was worth. Her ragged breathing blended with his and they leaped into the whirlpool together. Ahhhhh.

Reveling in the pulsing glory of their mutual climax, she shouted and swore at the top of her lungs. So did he. Their reaction was so over-the-top, so unchecked and bonkers that it eventually turned into laughter.

When she finally had enough air in her lungs that she was able to speak, she gazed down at him. "What was *that* all about?"

He smiled. "I think we finally remembered how to have fun."

"Could be." Damn, but he looked sexy right now with that satisfied smile on his face. "We used to have fun, didn't we?"

"All the time." He held her gaze. "Think about that while I take care of this condom."

"Okay." She carefully disengaged and he climbed out of bed, leaving her to ponder the situation.

She had no trouble tracing a path back to her first mistake — adopting those horses. It had seemed innocent enough. Her favorite author was a supporter of the program and she had fond memories of Luis.

A little too fond, obviously, since adopting the horses had clearly been the genesis for her dream. Her attempt to get rid of it had only made things worse.

If she could leave tomorrow, she'd minimize the damage. But taking Fudge away from a cozy barn and a skilled vet when he'd just begun to heal was a non-starter.

Luis came out of the bathroom. "I say let's stick this out. We can handle it."

"But a short while ago you were ready to call a halt."

"And then what? I didn't think it through. You'd still be here. We'd be miserable while wearing happy faces for the sake of everyone else."

"That sounds awful. But the more we make love—"

"The more fun we'll have. How about we focus on that?" The tension in his body was subtle, tightening his shoulders, etching a furrow between his brows.

She gazed at him. Such a beautiful man. Of course he'd haunted her dreams. And would likely be doing it more in the future after this weekend. She sucked in air and let it out. "If you're game, so am I."

His shoulders dropped and his mouth relaxed into a slow smile. "Great." His gaze held hers for a beat. "None of your stuff is here. I just realized that."

"Didn't even think of it."

"I'll take that as a compliment."

"You should."

"No worries. We can grab a few things in the morning."

"I'm not in love with the idea of parading down here in broad daylight with my stuff. How about now?"

"Now's fine." He stooped to pick up his briefs.

"I can do it. You don't ha—"

"I'm a gentleman. I'll help you carry. And protect you from grizzlies."

She gathered her clothes and started dressing. "You told me the fence keeps out predators."

"Damn, I did say that, didn't I? Well, since I promised to be straight with you, here's the truth. I want to go with you and make out on your inviting little bed."

"You just think you do. Compared to your ginormous king, it's cramped."

"That's what would make it fun. Like camping."

"You've camped in a trailer before?"

"No, always wanted to but never got around to trying it." He pulled on his jeans and shoved something in his pocket.

She paused to stare at him. "Did you just put a condom in your pocket?"

"Ah, you saw that."

"Are you serious?"

"This is the exact opposite of serious. This is unnecessarily complicated and crazy, which is why I want to do it." He picked up his shirt and shoved his arms into the sleeves. "You said we'd make love again tonight."

"You're insane." But the idea was growing on her, setting off a reaction in significant parts of her body.

He must enjoy the idea of making love in different venues. He'd had to give up on his barn plan so maybe this was scratching the same itch.

"Come on, be insane with me."

"Okay, sure. If that would make you happy." She put on her boots.

"It will." He circled the room blowing out votives. "And it'll make you happy, too. I guarantee it."

"'It won't be as private. I left all the windows open a couple inches to keep it cool. Closing them would make it stifling in there."

"I'm capable of being a quiet lover when required."

Anticipation tightened her core. The more he talked about this the more she was into it. She'd always known he was passionate. She hadn't known he also had a spirit of adventure.

As they walked back though the house, she took note of a beehive fireplace, a leather sectional facing it and a rough-hewn coffee table that held nothing but his laptop. A masculine and functional room.

Multi-functional, too? Now that she understood him better, she had no trouble imagining hot lovemaking on that sectional.

He ushered her out the door into a night made for lovers. She breathed in cool night air scented with pine. The half-moon sat lower in the sky adding sparkle to the stars overhead.

"It's beautiful here." She let out a sigh of pleasure.

He glanced at her as he took her hand. "*Si, chica bonita.*"

A blush warmed her cheeks. "You still get to me with compliments like that."

"And you still get to me just by existing. Five years hasn't changed my reaction."

"Same, here. In fact, seeing you surrounded by everyone and everything you love... you're damn near irresistible."

"Which leaves you some room to resist me, *querida*?"

"Clearly not much, since we're on our way to have sex in my trailer. I wouldn't have thought of that in a million years."

"Only took me about ten seconds."

"I hope you know what you're getting into. It's not easy maneuvering in there with two people."

"I realized that when I checked it out today. We'll have to get undressed in the living/dining area."

"You've been plotting this episode since then?"

"You betcha. I didn't know my opportunity would arrive this fast, though."

"Makes me wonder what else is going on in that imagination of yours."

"What can I say? You inspire me."

"I do?"

"You didn't know that? You don't know I think you're amazing?"

"I guess I do. I mean, we've had a pretty good time in—"

"That, too, but I'm saying in general. Talk about imagination and living your dream, you've accomplished a fudging miracle by—"

"Fudging." She laughed. "You said fudging." Which made her think of her horse. They should pay him a visit... but later.

"Yeah, I kinda like how it sounds. But to my point, you started with nothing except talent and grit and you've created the life you imagined. That's damned impressive."

"Thank you."

"I'm not surprised that you succeeded. I saw what you bring to the table. Your intuitive understanding of horses is rare and you're one of the most focused people I've ever met."

His extravagant compliments stole her breath. "That means a lot, coming from you. When I watched you in the arena, I figured if I could be even half as good—"

"You're kidding, right?" He stopped a few yards from the trailer and turned to her.

"Not kidding. You're the gold standard."

"I had the advantage of working with my dad for years. I should have skills. Unless you had a mentor you never told me about, you started from scratch. Which tells me you have a gift."

She stared at him as she struggled to accept such high praise. "If I have a gift, it's for hard work. That's what got me here."

"I'm not implying you don't work hard. I'm sure you do. But you also have a sixth sense about horse behavior and what it means. Everybody doesn't just naturally have that."

"Then why did I have to ask you if I should take the road down here fast or slow? I should have sensed what Fudge wanted."

"For one thing, you were stressed about him, about me, about imposing on my family. Nobody operates well at times like that. You also seem to think I know more than you, which isn't true, by the way."

"Of course it is. You just said you spent years being taught by your dad. I came late to the party. I couldn't fully throw myself into this until I could leave home and move in with Cole."

"Which makes my case. You're a phenom."

"That's—"

"You are, *querida*." He took her by the shoulders. "I could learn things from you. And while we're on the subject, I didn't think of this before because I was fixated on that cozy bed of yours. But we're right here next to the barn. We should go see Fudge."

"First?"

"Definitely."

"Some guys would want to proceed to the trailer and see the horse later."

"I'm not some guys."

"No, you certainly aren't." He was one of a kind. Leaving him would be the hardest thing she'd ever done.

21

Luis stood back so Jordan could have a private moment with Fudge. Also, he didn't see any point in putting himself in the picture, literally. Monty's cameras were cramping his style.

But he wasn't complaining. His brother had come through in the clutch, offering Jordan's precious horse a path to recovery.

When they'd walked in, Fudge had been on his feet, dozing with his eyes closed and the hoof of his bandaged right foreleg barely touching the floor. The wrapping still looked secure.

The gelding roused himself to greet Jordan, thrusting his muzzle against her chest and rumbling a soft greeting. Sweet.

Shoving his hands in his pockets, he encountered the condom he'd put there. He looked forward to making love with Jordan in her snug little bedroom. It would be fun.

But he'd rather not look too closely at his motivation, which might be more complicated than he was willing to admit. Hell, this entire setup was loaded with significance and he'd just sold her on the idea of keeping it light and breezy.

She probably didn't believe it any more than he did. But she was stuck here for now because of Fudge, so pretending they'd have a merry old time and part friends was the way to go.

Giving Fudge a last hug, she walked out of the stall, latched the door and walked toward him. "He said to tell you hello."

"I appreciate that." He took her hand and headed out of the barn. "How's he feeling?"

"Much better. He's relaxed and not anxious anymore. When we picked him up at the stable he was so worried, especially because I wasn't there. He's used to having me close by."

"Naturally. You always are." Yeah, he envied that animal.

"I guess that's the flip side of my setup. He depends on having me around."

"Nothing wrong with that. With your arrangement, you always will be." They passed her truck and paused at the steps into her living quarters. "Ladies first."

"I have an idea." Her voice was breathy.

"I have several."

"I'll just bet you do. Let me go in and get undressed. Give me a couple of minutes to get out of your way and then you come in."

"I don't mind playing bumper cars."

"Well, I do." Giving his hand a squeeze, she hurried up the steps and through the door, leaving it open.

Naturally she minded sharing a cramped space while they undressed. She'd grown up with one sibling instead of seven and cold, distant parents. She must really like him to allow him in that trailer at all.

He counted out the minutes, gave her a few extra seconds and went inside, closing the door behind him. Pretty dark in there. But it made sense that she didn't want to turn on lights in case someone might be awake and take notice.

He could still smell her shampoo, but the scent was lighter, now. The heady aroma of arousal, his and hers, took center stage, making his nostrils flare and his cock thicken.

The cave-like atmosphere excited him even more than he'd expected. He was clumsy as he peeled off his clothes. Gradually his eyes adjusted enough that he could see the padded bench on one side and the dinette seating on the other.

Leaving his clothes on the bench, he pulled the condom out of his jeans pocket and located the step-up into the bedroom.

A short climb left him in complete darkness. If he let go of the condom he'd never find it again. His breath hitched. "Which side are you on?"

"Neither. I'm in the middle."

Her sultry, intimate tone sent fire racing through his veins. Without sight, his hearing sharpened, picking up her rapid breathing and the whisper of her body moving against the sheet. Ripping open the condom package sounded like the whine of a buzz saw.

She responded with a low chuckle. "Not wasting any time, are you?"

"No, ma'am." Her laughter and comment helped him pinpoint her position. Tossing the wrapper over his shoulder into the main room, he stepped sideways along the narrow space between the foot of the bed and the wall.

Was this the middle? Seemed like it should be. "I can't see a thing. I don't want to put my knee on your foot."

"Come on down, cowboy. I've cleared the runway. You're free to land the plane."

The vivid invitation almost undid him. He couldn't say why darkness turned this simple position into an erotic adventure. But he trembled with eagerness as he slid between her open thighs.

Guided by her breathing, he braced his arms on either side of her, leaned down and feathered a kiss over her lips. His cock throbbed with impatience as he fought for control. When he could trust himself not to come, he lowered his hips and sank into her warmth.

She wrapped her arms around him with a sigh. "You made it."

"Barely." He clenched his jaw. "Hold still or this'll be over really fast."

"Having fun?"

"Big fun." He gulped for air. "Complete darkness is a turn-on. Who knew?"

"Not me."

Lowering his head, he kept his hips still as he nibbled on her mouth some more. "Enjoying yourself?"

"Uh-huh. Since I can't see, it's like I have more nerve endings."

"Right." He tested his self-control, easing back and gliding in again. Brushing his chest lazily over her taut nipples created an erotic tingle he might have missed if he'd been able to see her.

He did it again, savoring the friction, her quick little breath in response. "Ready to go for it?"

"Oh, yeah." She wrapped her legs around his. "So ready."

"Then hang on." He began to thrust, slow and steady at first, then zeroing in on her sweet spot and pumping faster.

He'd never made love to her without being able to look in her eyes. Without that, he tuned into her body, reacting to the way she arched into him with each stroke, intensifying the jolt of pleasure as the tip of his cock touched the back of her womb.

The tightening began, a gentle squeeze that gradually became stronger. The pressure grew in his balls as his climax shouldered its way forward.

She was panting now, gripping his glutes as the liquid sound of their movements increased the ache in his groin. Cocooned in the darkness, her legs entwined with his as he drove home again and again, they moved as one.

His ragged breathing synchronized with her rhythmic gasps. With her first spasm he let go, plunging up to the hilt. Boundaries disappeared as orgasmic waves overtook them, tossing them in the same warm, salty, rolling sea of release.

Pressing his mouth against her shoulder, he muffled a deep, heartfelt groan. She didn't cry out, but her fingers dug hard into his glutes as she quivered beneath him.

He didn't have to guess as to whether she'd had a good time. In the dark, absorbing every sensation, he knew her in a way that went far beyond the bond they'd shared five years ago.

He couldn't stop that bond from growing stronger even if he tried. And he didn't want to try. This was meant to be. If he only had three nights, he'd make every single moment count and consider himself a fortunate man.

Lifting his head he sought her lips and delved into her mouth with a kiss of deep gratitude. Her soft moan made him wish he'd prepared for more than one round.

He ended the kiss slowly, drawing away with reluctance. "I have to—"

"I know. Watch the steps."

"I will." He chuckled. "Can't afford to trip." He took his time leaving the bed and navigated the steps with great care.

The bathroom was a longer walk than he had to make in his house, but he figured that putting it at the front end allowed room for a decent-sized shower.

The layout was elegant and simple. Even though he could barely make out the fixtures, he didn't have to fumble around. He was becoming fond of this little house on wheels.

As he started back toward the bedroom, he paused. "Hey, Jordan," he called softly. "Maybe I should get dressed while I'm out here."

"Or you could come back and cuddle."

"Yes, ma'am." He took the steps like a pro this time around.

"I moved to the left. Your left."

"Got it." He climbed in and reached for her.

She snuggled against him, wrapping her leg over his thigh and pressing her breasts against his pecs. "I didn't know I'd like this so much."

"I should have brought more supplies."

"I never thought of inviting you to stay with me instead of me staying with you."

"We could, except we can't be loud here."

"Yeah, your place is better, and you don't have the tricky walk and the tiny bathroom."

"I didn't mind it. Even in the dark I could find everything because it's so well designed. That goes for the whole place. It's ingenious."

"I learned a lot with my first one, which I bought used. I had a detailed drawing to give the folks who built this."

"You created the layout?"

"Yep."

"Every time I turn around I find something else to admire about you."

"Good grief. You'd better ease up on the compliments. I'm liable to get full of myself and be impossible to live with."

"I can't imagine that." He combed his fingers through her hair. "Sounds like something that was said to you, though."

"My parents, of course. Specifically my mom. I ignored most of what she said over the years, but that one's on target. I have exacting standards. That can make a person hard to be around for any length of time."

"What about Cole? Didn't you live with him for a while?"

"Yes, but he's my big brother and he's so easy-going he'd put up with anything. I'm all he's got and vice-versa."

"You and I basically lived together for three days. I didn't find you impossible."

"Three days doesn't count."

"How about six days?"

"You can't go adding these three to those three."

"Sure I can. Six days is plenty of time if you're paying attention, and I am. I don't see you being a pain in the ass."

"You called me stubborn when I didn't want you going with me to get Fudge."

"That's not the same thing at all. In fact, you were trying not to be a pain. I was the pushy one in that scenario."

He wished to hell he hadn't called her stubborn. Her parents had probably used that word, too. *Dios mio.* Was this why she'd created a solo life on the road? If so, and he could change that damaging belief... he could change everything.

<u>22</u>

Jordan woke to sunlight and an empty spot where Luis had been. Damn, she'd fallen asleep while they'd been talking.

A piece of paper lay on the pillow next to hers.

Buenos dias, querida. My apologies for falling asleep. I'm either finishing up barn chores, in the shower, or in the kitchen making us breakfast. Come on down. If you're not there by eight, I'll knock on your door. XO, Luis

Scrambling out of bed, she hopped down the steps and located the clock on the microwave. Seven-ten. Not too bad.

She had no way to communicate with him since her phone was in her backpack and she'd left that in his casita. Might as well jump in the shower and dress for the day before walking down to his place.

Chances were good she'd meet somebody along the way. So what? The trailer was her home. Nothing strange about needing to pop down there to fetch a few things.

As she quickly showered, she tried to remember what they'd been talking about before she'd fallen asleep. Not the pain in the ass discussion. She'd steered him away from that.

Oh, yeah, childhood memories. She'd asked him about his first impressions of Laughing Creek at the tender age of four.

He'd been scared, but Spence Bridger was the hero of that story. His open-hearted delight in Mila, Luis and Zay had replaced their fears with excitement for a brand new adventure.

She'd told him about the tiny hut she'd built from scrap wood when she was six. Tucked into the woods adjoining her family's property, the hut had been her secret hideaway from everyone, even Cole.

Turned out Luis had built something similar at the same age. Reminiscing about their private hidey-holes must have made them both drowsy.

When had he left for barn duty? Could have been as early as five. He might have finished making breakfast by now, but at least she'd get down to the casita before he had to come fetch her.

Pulling on a favorite blue T-shirt with horses on the front, she chose a pair of jeans with some bling on the pockets and down the outside seam of each leg. She'd be meeting M.R. Morrison today.

She tossed yesterday's clothes in the bathroom hamper built into the wall. Luis claimed she was brilliant for designing this living space, but all it took was common sense.

Might as well grab her stuff and take it with her. No telling when she'd have time later.

Packing it quickly, she gave her hair one more pass with the brush before tossing it in with her other toiletries. She'd put on makeup before she left the casita.

She started out the door with the duffle and paused. She'd left the bed unmade, something she never did. It was a point of pride.

But it would take at least five minutes because the space was so tight. Luis had said he'd fix breakfast. He might even be stalling in hopes she'd show up.

Screw it. Nobody would see it besides her. She hurried down the steps and walked quickly past her truck. Should she look in on Fudge?

Not right now. She was all ready for the trip to town. Chances were good she'd have a few minutes to go see him before they left for the autograph party.

Nobody was in sight as she set out for the casita. She glanced toward the pasture where the horses had gathered around the slow feeder. Not much hay was left.

Since the horses weren't spending much time in their stalls, Luis's barn duty might have consisted of hauling hay out to the pasture and checking the water tank.

Five years ago she'd learned he had an ingrained habit of rising at dawn. Folks raised on a ranch usually did. She still had to set an alarm, as evidenced by how late she'd slept this morning without one.

As she approached the casita, Rio came out the front door and crossed the patio. He gave her a wave as he opened the gate. "Hey, Jordan! Luis told me to keep an eye out for you. He's in there making breakfast."

His greeting was matter-of-fact and casual, dispelling any potential awkwardness. "That's good. I was afraid I might be too late."

"No, ma'am, you're right on time. Nice outfit." He had Luis's smile.

"Thanks. I figure M.R. Morrison deserves a little bling."

"That's for sure. I've been looking forward to this for months. We all have." He held the gate for her. "I'm glad you're here for it."

"Me, too." He was an interesting blend of his mom and dad. She'd bet he'd inherited those electric blue eyes from Spence. The thick curly hair and the smile came from the Maldonado side. "See you soon."

"Yes, ma'am!" He tipped his hat and flashed her another smile.

Adorable. Made her chuckle. No wonder he had girls trailing after him.

The scent of spicy food drifted from the open window of the casita and Luis opened the door before she had a chance to.

She froze, dazzled by the sheer beauty of the guy — his strong jaw freshly shaved, his jet-black hair damp from the shower, his broad shoulders showcased by a snug white T-shirt and his narrow hips tucked into faded jeans. He was barefoot. And he smelled like heaven.

"There you are." His voice was a soft purr as his gaze swept over her. "Looking good enough to eat."

Lust curled and stretched in her core. "I could say the same."

He reached for her. "Get in here, you." Tugging her through the doorway, he took her duffle, dropped it on the floor and pulled her into his arms. "I've missed you."

"Missed you, too. Why didn't you wake me up?"

"You'd had a long day." Nudging the door closed with his foot, he gave her a slow, deep kiss that left her breathless and trembling. "I want you again," he murmured against her lips. "But breakfast's ready and your brother's called twice."

"Cole?" That news splashed cold water on the fire licking through her veins.

"Is there another Cole in your life?"

"How do you know it was him?"

"The second time your phone rang I dug it out of your backpack. That was the name on the screen and it was the same ringtone as before, *We Built This City*."

"Yeah, he loves that old song. I'd better see what's up. Must be important." She sorted through reasons for his calls, none of them good. He usually texted.

"Your phone's on the coffee table next to your backpack." He released her. "Should I dish us up?"

"Yes, please. Thanks for making breakfast." She walked around his massive leather sofa and picked up her phone. Once she tapped on it, she understood why he'd called twice.

He'd texted her last night. Under normal circumstances she would have answered, if not then, at least first thing in the morning.

She opened the text. *Hey, sis, did you know M.R. Morrison has a book signing in Mustang Valley tomorrow? I know you love her books. Don't know if you're available, but it would be fun to meet you there and catch up.*

Of course she wanted to see him. She always wanted to see him. But....

"Jordan?"

She glanced up from her phone.

Luis stood in the kitchen doorway with a spatula in one hand. "What happened? Didn't he answer?"

"I haven't called him yet. I just read his text from last night. He suggested meeting up at the signing today."

"Oh!" His hesitation was brief. "That would be great. I'd love to meet him."

"You would? Even if..." She trailed off, still not sure how she wanted to handle this unexpected turn of events.

"Even if that means we take that duffle back to your trailer? Yes, even then. Naturally I'd rather have you stay here, but... your brother, your choice."

The selflessness in that statement took her breath away. The taste of his passionate kiss still lingered. But he'd ignore his needs and plans if they would create an awkward situation for her.

When she considered how much she cared for both men in the equation, the decision became obvious. Neither of them were the type to play games.

Neither was she. "I'd like to invite him out to the ranch for the weekend, if that's okay."

"Absolutely. I'm sure Mom will offer to put him up."

"Or he can stay in my trailer."

"He can?" His gaze brightened, but then the glow faded. "Oh, that's right. You have a foldout bed, too. I forgot."

"I meant he can stay *alone* in my trailer."

"Yeah?" The sparkle returned.

"I'll tell him about us. Not on the phone, but after he gets here, when we have a chance to talk."

"Alrighty, then." His chest heaved.

"I assume our food's on the table."

"Yes, ma'am. Just waiting for you."

"I'll make the call a quick one. Then I'll have to eat fast so I can put fresh sheets on my bed before we leave for town. And check in on Fudge."

"I really want to kiss you right now, *querida*."

She smiled. "I promise you'll have plenty of opportunity to kiss me tonight."

"I'll hold you to that promise." He turned and walked back into the kitchen, giving her privacy for the call.

She felt like a trapeze artist performing without a net as she tapped her screen and Cole's phone started ringing. She'd thrown out her usual playbook with this move.

Instead she'd followed her instincts. Picturing Cole meeting Luis and the rest of the

Bridger Bunch generated warm fuzzies in her chest. She'd go with that.

23

Luis pulled away from the ranch at eight-forty-five and followed his mom's van out to the main road. Adam and Tracy had gone in early to set up the ribbon cutting ceremony taking place with the town council at nine-thirty.

Mila, Claudie, Greta, Grandma Doris and the aunties were tucked into the van. Mila had texted Jordan to ask if she wanted to go with them. He'd halfway expected her to do it. After all, she'd been a happy camper hanging out with that group yesterday.

Instead she'd replied with thanks and a smiley face, and said she'd be riding shotgun in his truck. And didn't he love that move.

Their dynamic had shifted. Ever since she'd decided to be open with her brother about their relationship, she'd taken ownership of it. She was no longer self-conscious about letting his family know she cared about him, either.

Having Monty, Zay and Rio in the back seat didn't keep her from reaching over and squeezing his arm or giving him an affectionate glance. He didn't kid himself this signaled a change in her plans, but it would be nice while it lasted.

He braced himself for some teasing comments from his brothers but they didn't make any. He appreciated their restraint. Instead they asked questions about Cole. Could he ride? Did he look like her? How tall was he? When was he getting to town?

Jordan ticked off the answers on her fingers. "He'll be here around one. He's six-three, has brown hair that gets blond streaks in the summer if he doesn't wear his hat. His eyes are gray and he wears glasses for reading. He rides whenever someone gives him the opportunity. He doesn't have a horse of his own."

"Then he should definitely ride while he's out at the ranch," Zay said.

"I'm sure he'd love to. He was planning to adopt a couple wild horses right after we hung up this morning, so Mila and Claudie want him to come along on the H&H tour."

"He can ride Whiskey," Rio said from his spot in the middle seat. "I'll be driving the wagon."

Monty glanced at him. "Since when are you driving the wagon? I thought Luis was doing that."

"Since this morning." He hesitated and leaned toward the gap between the two front seats. "Hey, *hermano*, can I tell them what we talked about?"

"Go right ahead. It's not a secret."

"Did you tell Jordan?"

"Didn't have a chance." He'd wondered if Rio would choose to bring up this topic. It would be better if Jordan heard it from Rio than from him.

He'd gotten his kid brother out of bed on purpose to see if he'd respond to an early morning text and agree to come down to the barn for a chat. If he was as ripe for a challenge as Auntie Kat had said, he'd make the effort.

He'd arrived in record time, a very good sign. He'd been groggy at first but once he'd heard the proposition, he'd become excited, even emotional, about the idea. He'd promised to work his ass off to become, in his words, an assistant horse whisperer.

But Rio didn't say all that now. His announcement was more straightforward. "Luis is giving me a shot at becoming his assistant."

"No shit." Monty sounded incredulous. "I mean, I'm sure you can—"

"No, you're not." Rio's matter-of-fact response wasn't the least bit defensive. "I'll bet Zay feels the same as you. I'm the last person you'd think of for that job."

Zay cleared his throat. "I wouldn't say that, but—"

"Look, he shocked the hell out of me, too. But the more I thought about it, the more I liked the idea. Maybe it won't work out. But I think it will."

Luis decided some embellishment was in order. "You two will be interested to hear that when I texted him at five a.m. he got out of bed and came down to the barn without asking questions."

Zay whistled in surprise. "That's amazing. I wouldn't have."

"Me, either." Monty laughed. "Unless a horse was in trouble I would have had several questions."

"But see, I knew he wouldn't text me at that hour if it wasn't important. And it was."

"I apologize for my initial reaction." Monty grimaced. "Not cool."

"No worries. It's just that everybody has their thing. Adam works with Mom on ranch stuff, Mila and Claudie have H&H, Greta's opening a coffee shop in the bookstore, you're a vet, Zay has his artwork. This could be my thing."

Luis felt Jordan's gaze on him. He glanced over at her but couldn't read her expression. Had she guessed this had something to do with her? If so, she'd be right.

He'd had two reasons for acting immediately on last night's suggestion from Auntie Kat. The timing was ideal. The wild horse barn was currently empty, which meant he and Rio could start fresh next week with a new set of two or three recruits.

But his other reason was all about Jordan. Despite what he'd said to Auntie Kat, he'd harbored a fantasy that ultimately she'd agree to take that job. This morning he'd deep-sixed his impossible dream by offering it to Rio.

As they reached the outskirts of town, conversation in the back seat turned to who from Rowdy Ranch would be at the bookstore when they arrived.

"I can't wait to meet Kieran's Irish granny," Rio said. "Kieran says she says more Irish stuff than he does, and he cracks me up with those sayings of his."

"I'm looking forward to the McLintock grandkids." Monty laughed. "Can you picture how they'll react to the second floor? I would have loved it when I was a kid, especially the tunnel and the revolving bookshelves."

"Hell, I love it now," Zay said. "I'm going through that tunnel and you can't stop me."

"There's a tunnel on the second floor?" Jordan glanced over her shoulder.

"Oh, right," Monty said. "I keep forgetting you haven't seen any of it. The second floor is all books and stuff for kids. Stuffed animals and puppets—"

"Don't forget the puppet theater," Zay broke in. "There's bean bag chairs and several child-sized rockers, and an entire wall is painted with chalkboard paint so they can draw on it."

"And it feels right that the upstairs is for kids." Rio leaned forward again. "I don't know if Luis has told you, but we used to play up there when we were little."

"I didn't know that."

"Wait'll you see it. There are four bedrooms and now there's a tunnel between the two on the right side of the hall and a revolving bookshelf between the two on the left."

"Wow. I might have to crawl through that tunnel myself. And draw on the chalkboard."

"Yeah, the chalkboard's my idea," Zay said, "but Adam gets credit for the tunnel. That was genius. Angie came up with the revolving bookcase."

Jordan turned toward the backseat. "Who's Angie?"

"The head of the crew that did the renovations. Also Desiree McLintock's only daughter."

"Oh, now I remember. She was mentioned in an M.R. Morrison newsletter. Did you guys spend a lot of time with the construction crew? You seem to know them pretty well."

Luis nodded. "We sure do. Whenever they worked several days in a row, they stayed at the ranch. We had a lot of fun dinner conversations."

"Do you think the whole family will show up?"

"We're about to find out." Luis took one of the few remaining parking spots in a large lot to the right of the stately Victorian.

"Get a load of the purple truck!" Zay opened his door to get a better look, letting in the lively music provided by the Mustang High pep band. "There's a custom paint job if I ever saw one."

"I'll bet it belongs to M.R. Morrison," Jordan said. "It looks like the one in a picture she had in her newsletter. She loves purple."

"She does?" Luis glanced at her. "Do you think that's why they painted the Victorian that color?"

"I did wonder when I walked out to see it Thursday night."

"I'd call it a good theory," Zay said. "Look at the house and look at the truck. They match, except for the difference in finish."

"I'll be damned." Monty unbuckled his seatbelt. "I was wondering who made that bold color choice. Looks like it was her."

"Or she floated the idea and Adam made it happen," Luis said. "He adores her."

"I seem to remember Grandma Lucy loved purple." Zay chuckled. "But not for a house."

"Times change." Luis reached for the door handle, thinking he'd help Jordan down, but Zay beat him to it. They all started toward the large crowd standing on the Victorian's circular driveway.

Zay and Jordan ended up in the lead and Luis debated whether to jockey for a position next to her. Then she fell back a few steps, putting her right beside him.

When she slowed, he automatically did the same until Monty, Rio and Zay were several yards ahead.

"This decision about Rio," she began, keeping her voice down. "I can't help but wonder if—"

"It wasn't my idea. Auntie Kat suggested it when we danced together last night. She wanted to dance with me so she could make her pitch. She's convinced he needs a purpose."

"Interesting. Do you think it'll work out?"

"I didn't when she first proposed it. I'm more hopeful after this morning."

"That's why I met him coming out of your casita."

"Yes, ma'am. We finished with the horses and still had more to talk about, so we came back to my place and had some coffee."

"Why didn't you tell me during breakfast? And don't say there wasn't time because there was."

"I thought it would be too pointed if I told you right away, as if I'd done the whole thing to prove I didn't have a secret plan to ask you to take the job."

"Did you?"

"Of course."

"I had a feeling."

"Not that it matters now, but I do think you'd be great at it."

"In theory. In reality, I'm—"

"Impossible to live with?"

She stopped and turned to him. "You haven't seen how I operate on a day-to-day basis. I'm exacting. I like my routine and I don't want anybody messing with it."

"Same here." He worked hard not to smile. He could have made the same speech. It was how he thought of himself.

But for the past twenty-four hours they'd had no routine at all and they'd survived just fine. Now wasn't the time to point that out.

He reached for her hand. "Come on. We don't want to be late for the ribbon-cutting ceremony."

"Dear God, no. I hate being late for special events."

This time he did smile. "Ditto."

24

Jordan wouldn't have described herself as the hand-holding type. But she enjoyed the sense of connection with Luis as they blended into the throng of several hundred people, including quite a few children. The high school pep band was rocking Jason Aldean's *My Kinda Party*, inspiring some folks to dance.

A large gold ribbon stretched across the base of the steps. Adam and Tracy were working the crowd along with five others, three women and two men, probably the town council. All of them wore *L'Amour and More Bookshop* branded T-shirts.

If this turnout was any indication, the bookshop would be a huge success. Who said people didn't read these days?

But clearly there were other factors at work besides just books. This stately Victorian represented a bygone era and no one except the Bridgers had been inside it for years.

A good marketing campaign would have made sure word got out about the renovations, especially upstairs. Kids had likely been begging their parents to bring them here for the grand opening. Zay would have to stand in line to wiggle through that tunnel.

A handsome-looking group stood on the Victorian's wide steps leading to the front porch. Jordan had no trouble recognizing Desiree McLintock, aka M.R. Morrison. Her picture was everywhere now.

She'd piled her copper-colored curls on top of her head, adding to her regal, *I'm in charge* vibe. What a powerhouse she was. How funny to think everyone had pictured a grizzled old cowpoke as the author of books about heroes and villains of the Old West.

Desiree had taken center stage along with her husband, Andy, a good-looking guy whose calm smile telegraphed kindness and strength. The number of adults and children fanned out on either side of Desiree and Andy. The McLintocks had prioritized this trip to Mustang Valley.

"Dollars to donuts that chickie-babe wearing the eye-catching flowered hat is the famous Irish granny we've been hearing about."

Jordan turned toward Kat, who'd quietly made her way over to Jordan. She was the one person who would describe a sweet-faced lady in her eighties as a *chickie-babe*, no doubt because she considered herself one. "What makes you think that's Granny?"

"Well, she's next to Kieran and he'd want to keep her close."

"Which one's Kieran?"

"He's on her right. The cowboy on her left is probably Rance McLintock, the new author in the family."

"I think you're right about Rance. He looks like the guy on the poster I saw when I walked out to the Victorian my first night in town."

"Take a look at that woman's flawless complexion. Eighty-something and not a line to be seen."

"Not from here, anyway."

"It'll still be true up close. That's the benefit of living in a place where every day is a spa day. I almost moved to the UK for that reason. Then I realized how much I'd miss this family. So Spence built me a little Swiss chalet and here I am, slathering on face cream every five seconds."

Luis leaned around Jordan and gave his auntie a smile. "You're gorgeous, *tia.* I don't see any lines."

"Then you need glasses, sonny-boy. But that's very sweet of you to say." She lowered her voice. "Good job, by the way talking to Rio. Nicely done."

"Thanks."

Her gaze moved past him to his three brothers. They were busy debating who was who in the Rowdy Ranch lineup and hadn't noticed her presence. "He called me. He's over the moon."

"I hope so. That would be a good thing."

"He's so looking forward to it, and I— oh, Jordan, I'm sorry, honey. How rude of me. Do you know what we're talking about?"

"I do. He told us on the way here that he'll be working with Luis. He's excited about it."

"I'm excited, too. Luis has broad shoulders, but he's only human. He's the only one training rescued horses for adoption now that Spence is gone and it's too much for one person."

"It's not that bad, *tia.*"

"It's just like you to say so, but you're desperately in need of a vacation. This break you're supposed to have over the Fourth isn't really time off since you took charge of the parade yesterday and you'll be on deck for tomorrow's H&H tour. All work and no play makes Luis a dull boy."

He chuckled. "You're exaggerating and you know it. Besides, I love what I do."

"I'm sure Jordan loves what she does, too. But clearly she values taking time out for having fun." She added a sly wink to that zinger. "Jordan, tell this guy it's okay to kick over the traces now and then."

Still blushing from the implications of that wink, she scrambled for an answer. "I'm the wrong person to give advice on that score. This weekend is my first one off in years. I'm either running a clinic or on the road to the next one. On non-driving or non-clinic days I give private lessons."

"Oh, dear. I had no idea, honey." She heaved a sigh. "Looks like you're two peas in a workaholic pod. I've a mind to get both of you non-refundable tickets to the Bahamas. But I promised I wouldn't interfere, so—"

Adam's voice came over the speakers mounted on either side of the steps. "Good morning, Mustang Valley residents and welcome visitors!" He'd ducked under the ribbon and taken a position a step below the McLintock clan. In addition to the mic, he held a gigantic pair of scissors.

He introduced himself and his fellow council members with a casual, irreverent style that had everyone laughing. Then his tone changed.

"This is a momentous day for all of us — the town, the council, and my family. My dad, Spence Bridger, dreamed of transforming his grandparents' home into something the whole town could enjoy. He also loved books, especially ones by M.R. Morrison. I wish—" His voice caught, and he paused to clear his throat.

"I wish he could be here to see this. Thanks to enthusiastic support from his favorite author and members of her family, specifically Lucky, the CEO of L'Amour and More, and Angie, whose crew handled the renovation, my dad's dream has come true. Welcome to L'Amour and More, the town's first bookshop!"

As the crowd clapped and cheered, Jordan swallowed past the emotion clogging her throat. Then she leaned close to Luis. "He's great at this."

He smiled. "Yeah. He is."

Adam gestured to the folks behind him. "As you can see, the McLintocks turned out in force for this event, which wouldn't be happening without their wholehearted participation. Let's give them a hand."

During the crowd's enthusiastic response, Jordan studied the folks on the steps. Desiree's daughter-in-law Oksana would also be signing today. Desiree had mentioned her a couple of times in her newsletter. But from this distance it was hard to say which dark-haired woman matched the publicity shot on the poster.

"I've asked Desiree to handle the ribbon-cutting honors," Adam continued. "After that, give us ten minutes for setup. We have a triple-threat autograph party for you — M.R. Morrison's newest *NYT* bestseller, *The Wayward Rider*, Rance McLintock's debut novel, *Tequila Shots in the Dark*, and Oksana Jones's second book in her bestselling series for tweens, *Odette Bidelspach Kisses a Boy*. Desiree, careful with these scissors. They scare the hell out of me."

Amid more applause and laughter, Desiree wielded the scissors, which turned out to be dull. Folks offered advice as she hacked her way through the ribbon. The pep band played the theme song from Jeopardy and a few people held up pocketknives in case she wanted to switch instruments.

When she finally cut through the last inch, everyone cheered and the pep band struck up the theme from *Rocky*.

"Ten minutes, folks!" Adam called out as he retrieved the scissors. Then he ushered Desiree and most of the McLintock family into the house.

But not all. Kieran and his granny came down the steps, their attention focused on the spot where Jordan stood. She quickly figured out they weren't targeting her.

They were headed straight for Kat, who turned and beckoned to Carmen, Ezzie and Doris. "Get over here! She's coming to meet the Damsels!"

"Hot damn!" Rio hurried over from the other direction. "I want in on this."

Jordan laughed. "Who wouldn't?" She glanced at Luis. "This family is a riot."

He gazed at her, the light in his brown eyes soft, his smile tender.

She forgot to breathe. How had she not seen this coming? But she had. She'd just chosen to ignore the signs. Now she had to face the truth.

He was in love with her. And that was bad. Very bad.

25

Big surprise, Jordan had fallen in love with the Bridger Bunch. Luis would have preferred that she'd fallen in love with him, but he'd take whatever advantage he could get.

If she'd bonded with his family, she'd have a tough time riding off into the sunset. Even if she did that on Monday morning, she'd come back. That gave him more hope than he'd had before.

It did seem like Fate that Adam's bookstore project had helped bring her here for the weekend. That gave her more reason to love the Bridger Bunch. They had an in with her favorite author.

And not just Desiree, but all the fascinating people in her orbit, like this Irish granny, for instance. He was as eager as the rest of them for this meeting between her and the Dazzling Damsels.

Kieran cleared a path through the crowd and glanced at Luis with a grin. He had to be relishing the moment, too.

Granny wasn't the only one who'd benefited from the Irish climate. Luis had never paid attention, but Auntie Kat's comments made him look closer. Damned if Kieran didn't look younger than him, and the guy was several years older.

Even his sad life didn't show on his face. He'd grown up an orphan with no kin except his granny until he'd found his half-brother Lucky McLintock a year ago.

Granny started talking the second she was within range. "Saints be praised! I get ta meet the Dazzlin' Damsels and the rest of the Bridger boyos!" The red, white and blue flowers on her hat bobbed as she hurried forward in her red, white and blue flowered dress.

Kieran made a megaphone of his hands. "Raquel! Mila! I've got my granny over here!"

"We'll be right there!" Mila shouted back.

Granny was puffing and pink-cheeked by the time she arrived. "Lookin'... lookin' grand, ya all are! And this?" She spread her arms to include the entire boisterous crowd. "'Tis good craic!"

Auntie Kat laughed. "I couldn't have said it better. It's a pleasure to finally meet you, Granny. Can I call you Granny?"

"'Course you can. I was plannin' ta call you Auntie Kat, 'cause that's how I learned it when I was studyin' up on the Bridger Bunch."

Auntie Carmen moved in. "You can call me—"

"'Tis Auntie Carmen, ya are. And she's Auntie Ezzie and she's Grandma Doris. I'd know ya anywhere." She switched directions. "And as for this lot...." She counted them off. "'Tis Luis, Rio, Zay, and Monty, right? Or did I get it arseways?"

Rio chuckled. "You nailed it, Granny. Good job."

"Thank ya kindly, lad." She beamed at them before turning to Jordan. "Studied pictures on my boyo's mobile, I did, ta help me sort out who was who. Guess he missed ya, luv."

"He wouldn't have had pictures of me. I got here Thursday night. I'm Jordan. I'm only visiting."

"Aha! Visitin' Luis, are ya?"

"Um, yes. Visiting Luis." She gave him a quick glance. "We go way back."

"Ah, reunited, ya are. That's grand."

Luis opened his mouth to correct Granny's assumption they were *reunited*. Closed it again. The word fit. For now.

"'Tis grand ta meet ya, Jordan." Granny's smile encompassed all of them. "Been hearin' about the Bridger Bunch since March. Yer legends, the whole lot of ya."

"We're *legends*." Auntie Ezzie clearly adored that label. "I really like this lady. She's *muy bueno*. Whatcha say, Luis. Can we keep her?"

"I think Kieran might not—"

"We're keeping him, Granny and Sara for tonight, at least." His mom joined the group. "Welcome, Granny. I'm—"

"Raquel. I know, luv. And here come yer girls, Mila, Claudette and Greta. Stunning, they are."

"I totally agree."

"Hey, Mom," Rio called out. "Did you just say they're spending the night?"

"That's the plan. I didn't have a chance to tell you all, but I contacted Kieran yesterday and suggested he, Sara and Granny stay at the ranch tonight and drive back tomorrow. That gives Granny's stomach a chance to settle before she's back on that road again."

"Did better'n I expected. Didn't boke at all. Stuck my head out the winda mosta the way, though. Made a bags of m'hairdo. Good thing I have a hat. Stayin' the night instead of drivin' back today is a blessin'."

Auntie Ezzie edged in her direction. "You should stay with us in the Dorm. We have an extra bed and you'd love it there, *mi amiga.* It'll be good craic, I promise. I'd invite Sara, except I can't remember who she is."

"Kieran's wife, Ezzie." Auntie Carmen gave her sister a look. "He showed us her picture. She's a beautiful redhead."

"Oh. Now I remember. *Perdon,* Kieran. But where is she?"

"Inside. She's part of the marketing team."

"Ah. Well, I doubt you two want to join us in the Dorm, but Granny can, right?"

"That's up to her."

"Spend a night in the Dazzlin' Damsels Dorm? Only an eejit would say no to that!"

"Hey, guys," Monty said. "They just opened the doors. The line's forming for the book signing. Should we get in it?"

"Ya should." Granny turned around. "Ya want all three books, especially Rance's. I'm in it."

Kieran grinned. "She's so in it. I'm prejudiced, but I think she steals the show. Listen, go ahead and queue up. Granny and I already have signed books so we're going upstairs. I want her to see what we did up there."

"I want to see that part, too," Jordan said. "We could wait and get our books signed after the line gets shorter."

"I like that plan." Monty started toward the front steps. "I've seen the upstairs, but not when little kids are in it. Well, except for Kendall's little girl, Jodie."

"I'm fine with going up there first." He'd follow wherever Jordan led. "Mom, I know you wanted to see the upstairs with kids in it."

"I do. Let's do that and get our books signed later."

"I'm not so sure we should wait, Mom." Greta looked worried. "There are so many people. What if they run out of books before we get there?"

"They won't sweetie. Since we provided the building for the bookshop, Lucky's put back enough for all of us."

"Oh! Great! Then I want to go upstairs with the rest of you."

"Maybe I should stand in line, though," Jordan said.

"No worries." His mom gave her a smile. "You're covered. I texted Lucky this morning to add books for you and your brother."

"Wow. Thanks. Thanks so much."

Granny nodded in approval. "Good on ya, Raquel, lookin' out for yer son's *cailin.*"

Although his mom blinked at the unfamiliar word, she didn't miss a beat. "It's what we do, right?"

"Aye, 'tis. Are we goin', then? I want ta see if I fit through that tunnel ya made, Kieran!"

As the group started walking toward the Victorian's wide steps, Luis took Jordan's hand.

She glanced up at him. "What's a *cailín*?"

"I'm not sure, but I'll bet holding hands is involved."

"Does your mom know what it means?"

"Nope."

That made her chuckle. "She's so cool."

"Yes, ma'am. She likes you, too."

"Did she say that?"

"She doesn't have to. I can just tell. Everybody likes you. You're a hit."

"I like all of them, too. I envy you growing up in this family. It must be wonderful, knowing you're part of the Bridger Bunch."

"It is wonderful." He hesitated. "We're always open to taking in new members." Might be the wrong thing to say, but he couldn't resist.

She paused at the base of the steps and turned to him. "I would absolutely come back to visit, but it wouldn't be fair to you."

His chest tightened. "Don't worry about me."

"I can't help it." She lowered her voice. "You're in love with me."

He sucked in a breath. *Deny it, fool!* He couldn't. She had him dead to rights.

26

Jordan instantly regretted those words. The panic in Luis's eyes cut her to the quick. "I'm sorry. Wrong time. Wrong place."

"Let's fix that." He tugged on her hand, leading her away from the steps and toward the far side of the house.

"Hey, you guys!" Rio called out. "You can't get in that way! Adam told us all the doors except these are locked!"

She glanced back. Rio was beckoning to them. "Listen, maybe we should—"

"We need to talk."

"Let 'em be, little brother." Monty hustled him up the steps.

"Luis, I'm sorry. I didn't mean to break up the party. I—"

"Not your fault. I started it." His voice was tight. "It's fine." He reached the corner of the building and ducked around it. "There's a place. It's through that break in the hedge."

She followed where he led, turning sideways to fit through the narrow space between a couple of sweet-smelling hedges. "I guess you would know the area."

"Like the back of my hand." A wooden bench, gray with age, sat almost hidden under the hanging branches of a willow. Parting the branches, he ushered her through. "Want to sit?"

"Sure." She put her backpack on the bench and settled down on warm wood smoothed from years of backsides resting on it.

He sat beside her, his thigh brushing hers, his hands clasped loosely between his knees, his attention focused on the willow branches swaying gently in the breeze. Taking off his hat, he laid it beside him and ran his fingers through his hair.

The greenery muted the sounds of the crowd. Above them, birds chirped and fluttered. This would be lovely if she hadn't just dropped a bombshell. She waited, heart thumping.

He cleared his throat. "I am in love with you. I was pretty far gone five years ago, but I convinced myself it wasn't the real thing." He turned his head, his gaze steady. "This is."

She gulped. "I'm so sorry I dropped into your world and made a mess of things."

"Please don't be. This is my problem, not yours. I'm in love with you and you're in love with my family. I'm happy that you've made a connection with them. I hope you'll feel free to come back any time you want."

"But—"

"I can handle it. Who knows? Maybe next week some amazing woman will show up and sweep me off my feet."

"That would be terrific. I hope it happens." She hated the idea, which proved what a lousy person she was.

He smiled. "You don't much care for that concept, do you?"

"I do! I want you to find someone else!"

"No, you don't. You looked like you'd just tasted something nasty."

"Maybe I don't like the idea right now, but I will when it happens."

"I think you're a little bit in love with me, *querida*."

His sweet tone turned her insides to goo. "Of course I am. But I'd make your life miserable. You think you want me, but you really don't."

"Oh, I want you. No doubt about that."

"You don't want the person I'd become if we were together twenty-four-seven."

"You keep saying that, but when exactly does this impossible-to-live-with woman take over? I have yet to see her."

"You'd for sure see her if I gave up traveling and held all my clinics at the ranch. I love driving here and there. When I was little that was all I could think about, being on the move, seeing new sights."

"Why couldn't you do both? I'm not that needy. Some time at the ranch, some time on the road. Why not?"

"And what if we had kids? I assume you want them."

"We'd work it out. Do you want kids?"

She wasn't prepared for that question. "I don't see myself having any."

"That's not what I asked."

"If I could figure out how to have a child and keep the work I love, then, yes. Have kid, will travel. I can't believe you'd go for that scenario."

"It's not how I've imagined parenthood, but it's not a game changer. I'm flexible."

"Luis, I'm the wrong person for you, but you're blinded by love."

"Maybe I am." He cupped her face in both hands. "But where you see stumbling blocks I see a path to happiness."

"Because you're besotted." And in this idyllic spot she was falling under his spell. She couldn't stop herself from sliding her hands up his warm chest and gripping his strong shoulders.

His eyes darkened. "I love it when you touch me."

"I can't seem to help myself."

"We could make it. I know we could. Just give me a little more time." He leaned closer, his lips almost touching hers. "Before you know it, you'll fall completely in love with me."

"That's what I'm afraid of."

"Don't worry. I'll catch you." His gentle kiss devastated her more than any of the hot passionate ones he'd given her in the past. This was the kiss of a man in love.

We Built This City blasted from her backpack, shattered the moment. She pulled away, shaking and disoriented. "My... my brother."

"Better answer it." His voice was husky.

"Right." She fumbled for her backpack and almost knocked it off the bench. Reaching inside it, she grabbed her phone and tapped the screen. "Cole? Is everything okay?"

"Just ducky, sis! I got on the road earlier than expected and I'm standing in front of a purple Victorian looking around for you. Are you inside?"

"No, no. I'm—" She looked at Luis. "Stay there. I have someone I want you to meet."

"Oh, you do, do you? Don't tell me my little sis found herself a boyfriend this weekend."

"I guess you could say that, but it's... complicated."

"It always is. Listen, did I interrupt something? I can hang out here if you need to—"

"We'll be right there." She disconnected. "Do I look kissed?"

"Sadly, you don't. Want me to give it another shot?"

"No!" She stood, picked up her backpack and shoved her phone inside. "We'll look suspicious enough as it is, creeping around the corner of the house."

"I wasn't planning to creep." Getting to his feet, he put on his hat.

"You know what I mean. Clearly we were back here doing something."

His dimples flashed. "I should hope so. If we were wandering around in the bushes for no reason, that would be a cause for concern."

"Do I have any leaves on me from the hedge?"

"No leaves." His eyes sparkled with amusement. "No damning evidence whatsoever. Except the creeping out of the bushes part."

She laughed. "Okay, I'm being ridiculous. It's just that I was going to lead up to telling him about you, but I can't exactly do that now. Let's go meet my brother." She pushed through the branches of the willow.

"So that's the plan?" He followed her. "You're going to march up to him and tell him we're sleeping together?"

"Not like that, but sort of. I mean, there's no point in beating around the bush." She sidestepped through the narrow opening again.

"Or the hedge."

"Ha-ha. Do I have leaves on me now?"

"Just one." He plucked it off her back.

"So do you." She brushed it off his chest and they kept walking. He made no move to hold her hand, which was probably just as well.

"Is Cole the protective type?"

"Does a bear poop in the woods?"

"Not in our woods. We have an electric fence."

"Cole's not aggressive, if that's what you're asking."

"That's what I'm asking, since you're going to straight out tell him we're doing the mattress mambo. Does he work out?"

"Doesn't need to. He's in construction."

"In other words, he could flatten me."

"He's not going to flatten you." She checked the area around the circular drive. "He said he was standing in front of the house, but that's not very specific."

"It's a big house."

"I should be able to see him from here." She walked around the corner of the house. "There he is! Right by the steps!" Joy flooded through her and she walked faster. "Cole! Over here!"

"Hey, Jordie!" His long strides ate up the distance and a huge smile lit up his beloved face.

Made her heart ache. How had she let so much time go by? She ran the last couple of yards and he scooped her up, laughing as he swung her around.

"How the fudge is Fudge?" He set her down.

"Healing. It's good to see you."

"Same." He took a breath. "It's been too long."

"It has. Let's not ever go this long again."

"Let's not. You look great."

"You, too."

He glanced over her shoulder. "Hey, there, friend. I'll take a wild guess you're the one she wants me to meet."

"I am." Luis stepped forward and offered his hand. "Luis Bridger."

"Cole Sterling."

She moved to one side as the two men eyed each other.

Cole nudged back his Stetson. "In case you can't tell, my sister is fudging important to me."

With a deadpan expression, Luis pushed on the brim of his hat with his forefinger. "She's fudging important to me, too."

Cole stared at him, and then he started laughing. "She told you."

"She did."

"Hell's bells, Jordie! What else did you tell him about me?"

"That was it. Seemed like it was your profile in a nutshell."

"Guess that's about right." He studied Luis. "How long have you known my sister?"

"Technically five years."

"Five years?" He looked at her. "How come I've never heard about him?"

"We met at a clinic five years ago. Then we lost touch until I decided to come to Mustang Valley for the weekend and we… reconnected."

He held her gaze. "I see. Lucky my shotgun's in the backseat of my truck."

Luis snorted. "You'll have to point it at her. She refuses to make an honest man of me."

"Can't say I'm surprised. She's always been tough to pin down." He turned to her. "So what's wrong with this guy, Jordie? Snores too loud? Won't pick up his socks? Leaves the toilet seat up?"

"It's way worse than that. He's delusional."

"Is that true, Bridger?"

"You be the judge. She insists we wouldn't make it for the long haul because she's impossible to live with. But she has yet to prove it, so I'm calling bullshit."

"Hm. This sounds like a discussion the three of us should be having over a beer after this event is over."

"I'm game. Jordan?"

"I'm thinking." She hadn't known what to expect from this meeting of her brother and Luis, but instant friendship between the two men had never occurred to her.

It should have. She'd naturally be attracted to someone who shared characteristics with Cole. And at this point she felt outnumbered.

But there was a solution. "I'm up for that on one condition. I get to invite Mila."

"Mila. That name sounds familiar."

"She and her sister Claudette head up Hearts & Hooves. She knows Luis and she understands where I'm coming from."

Her brother nodded. "Sounds good. Now let's go check out this book signing."

"First we have to go upstairs to the kiddie section. They put in a tunnel and a revolving bookcase."

"What the fudge? We gotta go see that." He lit up, reminding her of the imaginative boy who'd been her lifeline growing up.

Her throat tightened. No matter how this weekend turned out, she'd be forever grateful for this poignant reminder that she needed to spend more time with her brother.

27

Luis had figured on liking Jordan's brother, so their instant connection hadn't surprised him. But he hadn't factored in the benefit of Cole's knowledge and insight. Jordan's brother might turn out to be a lifesaver. Or a nail in his coffin. Time would tell.

In any event, the guy hadn't punched him in the face. That was a good start. Cole's eagerness to see the kiddie section of the bookstore with its tunnel and revolving bookshelves spoke well for him.

The three of them headed up the Victorian's winding staircase with Jordan in the lead. Luis had stepped back so Cole could follow her. Observing the dynamic between brother and sister would likely give him valuable info about Jordan.

Judging from the giggles and squeals of joy coming from the upstairs rooms, Angie McLintock's crew had created a child's paradise. He'd seen it a couple months ago when it was almost done, but he'd missed the final walkthrough week before last.

It had been scheduled for the day a couple wanted to finalize their adoption of Batman and

Robin, mustangs he'd been working with since late February. Saying goodbye to those two had been tougher than any he'd trained so far.

Early on, his dad had warned him about that downside. Turned out it was worse without a buddy who shared his tug of grief when the horse trailer pulled away. Would Rio be a help in that regard? Would be nice if he was.

Speaking of Rio, that was his laugh, sure as the world. And Monty's voice. And Granny's. Was the whole gang still up here?

"There ya are, luv!" Granny called out when Jordan topped the stairs. "Wondered where ya got to, I did. Who's that fella with ya?"

As Jordan introduced Cole, more of his family popped into the hallway. They formed a knot around Jordan and Cole that stranded him one step below them. Leaning on the banister, he enjoyed the show.

Jordan's obvious pride in her big brother was fun to see. As for Cole, he had the makings of a UN diplomat. He joked and laughed with everyone as if he'd known them all his life.

Amazing, since he'd experienced the same unloving childhood environment as Jordan. Or maybe he'd had favored status as a boy.

His mom once told him she'd married Spence Bridger partly because he treated Claudie the same as Adam and Monty. Mila wouldn't become a second-class citizen in the Bridger household.

"Ya need to come see what Kieran, Angie and Kendall made." Granny stepped back and the group separated enough that Jordan and Cole could move forward. "'Twill make yer eyeballs bulge out."

Then she spotted Luis. "Back there all the time, were ya? Thought we'd lost ya down a hole."

"No, ma'am. Not a chance."

"Come on, then. There's a clatter of wee chiselers, but ya might get a chance ta go through the tunnel."

"A clatter of wee chiselers?"

Rio chuckled. "Means a bunch of kids, *hermano*."

"Kids up to no good?"

"No, just plain kids. Chiseler doesn't mean what it does over here. I'm getting in the swing of this Irish stuff."

"Hey, how's it going up there?"

Luis glanced down the stairs. The cowboy standing on the bottom step reminded him of Kieran. "Fine, I think. Haven't been in to see for myself." Had to be Kieran's half-brother, but damned if he could remember the guy's name.

Kieran came to the top of the stairs. "You should come up, bro. Everybody loves it."

"Believe I will." He took the steps two at a time. When he reached the landing he held out his hand to Luis. "Lucky McLintock."

He grasped the guy's hand. "Luis Bridger."

"I don't think you were at the walkthrough."

"I had something else I had to do that day so I missed it. Can't wait to see how everything looks."

Kieran gestured toward the first door on the right. "Get on in there. I'm heading across the hall. You need to come see that, too."

"I will." Luis glanced at Lucky as they started toward what he thought of as the tunnel room. "Must be fun to have your mom, your brother and your wife publishing books."

"It's a bookseller's dream. On top of that, Kieran and Granny moved here from Ireland last year, and now we're opening this amazing venue. My mom sure gave me the right name."

"Get teased about it much?"

"All the time. Couldn't care less." He motioned for Luis to go in first.

He didn't see Jordan, Cole or Granny but he spotted the tunnel opening, which looked big enough for them to have made it through. Too bad he'd missed that.

Lucky surveyed the area with a smile of satisfaction. "It's working exactly the way I hoped it would."

"It's a perfect space for kids." Primary colors of red, blue, yellow and green dominated the area filled with low bookshelves, bean bag chairs, building blocks and a menagerie of plush animals.

The chalkboard wall had attracted a lot of artists. Most of the drawings were stick figures and square houses with smoke coming out the chimney. But the elaborate horse had to be Zay's work.

Lucky's phone pinged and he checked the screen. "I need to get back downstairs. Good meeting you, Luis." He shook his hand again. "I'll see you at lunch over at the Raccoon, right?"

"I'll be there." After Lucky took off, he studied the tunnel again. He didn't absolutely have to go through it. Except Jordan must have or she would have passed him coming out the door. Same with the others, including Cole and Granny.

A small child crawled through, turned around and came back. Made it look easy. But that kid was less than three feet tall.

Just as Granny had said, the place was a clatter of wee chiselers. Some were local. He recognized them and their parents, who mostly stood back and let the kids enjoy themselves.

One bunch orbited around a little redheaded girl. When she called out the name Jodie, a small blonde girl responded.

He knew that kid. Her mom Kendall was the third member of Angie's crew and she'd often bring Jodie to the jobsite and then to the ranch when the crew stayed overnight.

The redhead was clearly in charge of her posse, ordering them around by name. Besides Jodie there was Susie, another blondie about Jodie's size, and Zach, a quiet brown-eyed boy.

Zach was similar in age to the ringleader but completely under her thumb. Evidently she expected him to monitor a baby girl crawling around on the carpet while she kept track of a baby boy about the same age.

A tall cowboy stood watching the dynamic. Something about his proud papa expression told Luis he was the redhead's dad. The guy met Luis's gaze and walked over. "Are you Luis Bridger, by any chance?"

"Guilty as charged."

"I'm Beau McLintock." He offered his hand. "Been wanting to meet you. I was talking shop with Jordan a while ago and she raved about your training methods." He checked on the kids and then turned back to Luis. "She predicted you'd show up soon."

"You're a trainer?"

"Yessir. But I've never dealt with a wild one. Read Buck Brannaman's book, though. Is your method anything like that?"

"I use some of his elements, some of my own."

"I'd love to tag along sometime."

"I'll bring in a new batch soon. I'd be glad to let you know, see if you're available."

"Great." He focused on the kids again.

"Is that redhead yours?"

"Yep, that's Maverick. We call her Mav. The little dude crawling toward the tunnel is her brother, Drew. He won't get far."

"Nope. She's on it. And the other baby?"

"Zach's sister Elvira. There would be one more rugrat, but Matty has a cold. I promised to watch everybody, which isn't too hard since I have Mav. She loves directing traffic and they all listen to her."

"They sure do. I think you have a future world leader right there."

"That wouldn't surprise me. Whatever she does, she'll be a force of nature just like her mother and her Grandma Dez."

"My mom's a little jealous of your mom on account of all these grandkids."

"Ah, they'll show up. Takes time."

"That's what we tell her. By the way, did you happen to notice if Jordan went through that tunnel?"

He grinned. "She did. Her brother, too, after Granny showed them how it was done."

"Guess I'll catch up with her."

"Goin' through the tunnel?"

"I think I have to."

His grin widened. "Yeah, you do." He turned back to the four kids who'd begun stacking colored blocks into a tower. "Mav, Uncle Luis is going through the tunnel. He could use some pointers."

Uncle Luis? Had he just been adopted into the Rowdy Ranch gang?

"Sure, Daddy!" She hopped to her feet, raced over and took him by the hand. "Don't be scared, Uncle Luis. It's easy."

Apparently Maverick was fine with adding him to her list of uncles. So was he. "Thanks, Mav. You've been through it, right?"

"Lots of times. You'll be fine." She led him over to the opening, an upside-down U shape.

"He'd better take off his hat." The boy with the big brown eyes had joined them. Jodie and Susie stood behind him.

Jodie gave him a smile and a wave, but Susie eyed him and shook her head. "He's too big."

"No, he's not," Mav said. "The others made it. Even my daddy made it." She gazed up at him. "You're too big to crawl on your hands and knees. Just flop down on your tummy. Pretend you're a seal."

He lowered himself to the floor and ignored the muffled laughter from the adults in the room. More kids arrived and crowded around him.

Mav waved her arms. "Move back. You'll make him nervous."

They all stepped back. Impressive.

"Okay, Uncle Luis. Hold your hat in front of you and pretend you're a worm."

"I thought I was a seal?"

"That's for the first part. Now you gotta be a worm."

"Or a snake?" He liked that image better.

"Snakes slide. But you'll kinda stick to the rug. You need to be a worm. Worms wiggle."

Couldn't argue with that logic. "Then here goes." Holding his hat in front of him, he began inching forward, wiggling like a worm. He tried not to think about how it looked from above.

"Come on, everybody!" Mav called out. "Cheer him on. Go, Uncle Luis! Go, go, go, go, go!"

Childish voices were quickly joined by adult ones. Except the adults had trouble cheering because they were laughing so hard. Beau had set him up for this. Too late he remembered Kieran had told stories about Beau McLintock, the family jokester.

Could he have quietly slipped through the tunnel without attracting any attention? Probably not. But he would have liked to try.

Damn, it was hot. And now the laughter was in stereo mode. More was coming from the opening ahead of him. He had a welcoming party.

When his boots cleared the far end and his head was inches from the opening on the other side, Jordan's face appeared, cheeks pink, blue eyes sparkling. "Can I take your hat?"

"Please." He held it out and kept wiggling. "Did you get this treatment?"

"I sure did. Having fun?"

"No."

She grinned. "Your face is red."

"No kidding. It's a hundred and fifty degrees in here." He worked his shoulders free and tried to get his knees under him, but his butt hit the top of the tunnel.

Dragging himself the rest of the way out, he stood, pulled out his bandana and mopped his face while his nearest and dearest cracked up. He gazed at Monty, Zay, Rio, Jordan, Cole and Granny. "One of you could've texted me a warning."

Monty shook his head. "No, we could not. We suffered through it. Figured you should, too."

"'Tis a rite of passage, it is." Granny beamed at him. "Ya conquered the tunnel."

"My hero." Jordan gave him a quick kiss on the cheek.

That felt damned good. Almost made up for the discomfort and humiliation.

"Well done, dude." Cole grinned and reached out a hand.

Cole's congratulatory handshake was welcome, the gleam of approval in his gray eyes even more so. Wiggling through that kiddie tunnel might have won him an ally.

28

The lunch hour tested the limits of the Raccoon's staff. A second wave of out-of-towners who'd come for the autograph party had added to the Fourth of July visitors who were staying through the weekend.

Looking for a way to give Desiree some privacy to enjoy her meal, Clem had petitioned the town council for permission to block off the street on his side of the square. That allowed him to set up tables in the street for those who weren't connected to either Rowdy Ranch or the Bridger Bunch.

The extended McLintock family and the Bridger Bunch combined brought the number inside to more than fifty. Mila and Claudie lobbied to include their H&H supporters and generously included Cole. Adam added the town council and each of them were allowed to bring a plus one.

Jordan had lucked out by somehow coming through the door with Desiree and her husband Andy. She'd gushed about Desiree's books and didn't regret a moment of doing that. Desiree's response had been as kind and down-to-earth as she sounded in her newsletter.

The four-top Jordan ended up sharing with Luis, Cole and Rio wasn't far from the six-top where Desiree and Andy sat with Adam, Tracy, Lucky and Oksana. Raquel was hosting a table nearby with Rance, his wife Lani, Mila, Claudie and Granny.

Jordan kept sneaking glances over at both tables, since she was also fascinated by Rance and Oksana. Although she'd been a voracious reader ever since she'd discovered books at an early age, she'd never met a published author in person.

Now three of them were only steps away. She'd identified which dark-haired lady was Oksana and which one was Angie. Easy to tell once she'd found out Angie was six months pregnant.

Luis gave her a smile. "Somebody has stars in her eyes."

"I can't believe I just talked to M.R. Morrison. I started reading him, I mean her, when I was a kid!"

"So did we. It never crossed our minds we'd meet this person. We didn't expect to see authors face-to-face."

"Probably because most of them were dead already," Rio said. "And we thought M.R. Morrison was some old guy who hated being around people."

"Well, I haven't read anything by her," Cole said. "But now I will. Any woman who can raise ten kids on her own while writing anything, let alone fudging bestsellers, has my attention."

"You'll like 'em," Luis said. "Lucky has her first one in stock. I'd recommend starting there. The hero's named Skye, the same as her oldest son."

"That's cool. I talked to him today. Okay, I'll get that one while I'm here, but I might start my reading program with Rance's book since it's got Granny in it. She's a hoot. And as it happens, I have more reading time now."

"Oh?" That got Jordan's attention Something in his voice told her it wasn't an idle comment. "Did they cut your hours at work?"

"I cut my hours. Cut 'em down to zero. I quit."

She blinked and straightened in her chair. "Wow." He quit? "I thought you liked it there."

"I used to. But lately I've felt sort of like I'm on a hamster wheel."

She had trouble processing that statement. He'd always said a steady job gave him a sense of security. "Well, if I know you, you have a plan."

"Actually, I don't. I was talking to Angie and she offered me a job, but I don't know if I'm ready to work for somebody else again."

Who was this guy and what had he done with her brother?

"I'm sure she could use you," Luis said. "Especially when she has that baby in October. She's good people. Kieran and Kendall adore her."

"I believe it. She seems great. I love that she and Dallas have already named their kid Montana before they know whether they're having a boy or girl. And don't wanna know until the day. Fudging brilliant."

"Yeah, but I would want to know," Jordan said. "I'd be dying of curiosity."

"But waiting builds suspense for the big day," Rio said. "I like that idea."

Cole nodded. "Me, too."

"I'd want to know." Luis glanced at her. "Why not find out? Makes planning easier."

"That's what I say. We have the technology so why not use it?"

"Right. We get enough surprises to deal with."

His glance in her direction felt like a warm hug, as if he'd sensed that Cole's news had thrown her for a loop. His understanding calmed her, which was ironic. Cole used to be the one she counted on for that.

She turned to her brother. "What about your apartment? Did you keep that?" His two-bedroom in Helena was nothing special, but it was the closest thing to a real home she'd ever had until she'd bought her custom trailer.

"The lease is up next month, so I need to make some kind of decision before then. I will. I just need time to think about things."

"I'm sure you'll figure it out." Yeah, having her rock steady Cole questioning his life path was uncomfortable as hell.

But this wasn't about her, was it? If he needed emotional support she was there for him. Or financial help, for that matter. She was solvent enough she could offer that, too.

Their food arrived and the conversation switched to Rio and Luis's next steps with the wild horse training program. Cole looked relieved to be talking about something else.

After lunch, Jordan excused herself to go check with Mila and find out if she'd be available to come back to the Raccoon after the afternoon autographing and chat with her, Luis and Cole.

She made her request quietly, but Granny looked her way. Was she lip-reading? She had hearing issues, which often made people better at reading lips.

Mila readily agreed to the meeting. Excellent. Now she could just slip away.... Or not. Granny beckoned her over.

Walking around to her chair, she crouched down so they were at eye-level. "What's up?"

Granny leaned close and lowered her voice. "'Tis an engagement party yer plannin'? Or a weddin'?"

"Neither one."

"But it hasta be. Yer brother and his sister. They're the ones yer goin' ta need fer the ceremony."

"There's no ceremony in the works. We're just going to talk."

She smiled. "Ah, yer slaggin' me, luv. I know what yer doin', I do. Go on and have yer *conversation*." She made air quotes. "The truth will out soon enough."

No use fighting it. "Tell you what. I'll fill you in on the details when we get back to the ranch."

"That would be grand."

The Raccoon emptied out and Rio rode back to the Victorian in Luis's truck, hopping in the backseat with Cole. Did Luis realize how much Rio idolized him? Kat had done a good thing by advocating for this new arrangement.

While Luis searched for a parking spot, she checked out the situation at the Victorian. The double doors were propped open again and lines for Rance and Desiree already stretched into the circular drive. If Oksana had one, it was contained within the house.

"Hey, guys, I was hoping for shorter wait times this afternoon, but that's not what I'm seeing."

Luis slid his truck into one of the last remaining spots. "I say we get our books and pick a line."

She nodded. "I agree. Do you know where the books are stored?"

"I had a chance to ask Lucky when we first went into the Raccoon, while you were talking to Desiree. They're in the kitchen. In the pantry."

"Do you know if he included any of Oksana's?"

"He set aside some of hers, too. He knows it won't be in high demand because it's not a Western, but he said she's a great writer."

"She is. I bought the first one because Desiree promoted it in her newsletter. It was terrific. I was a miserable tween girl so I can relate."

"I was a miserable tween boy," Cole said, "and I have no desire to revisit that time in my life."

Rio snorted. "Same here."

"I dunno, guys." Luis glanced toward the back seat. "Lucky told me he's enjoying that series. The books help him understand where his wife is coming from."

"Makes sense for him," Rio said. "He's in love with the author. If Sophie writes a book, I'll read that."

Cole laughed. "Let me guess. Sophie's your girlfriend."

"For now, anyway. We like each other but it's not serious."

"Good for you. Take your time. Anyway, I'm sticking with Desiree's and Rance's books. But what's this about a stash in the kitchen? How are we supposed to pay for them?"

Luis glanced over his shoulder. "You're not."

"That's ridiculous. The authors should get paid. Besides, some of the proceeds go to Hearts & Hooves."

"You're welcome to make another donation to H&H if you want, but the McLintocks are giving us these books as a token of their gratitude."

"For what, exactly?"

"The Bridger Foundation is renting them space at a very reasonable rate. We also paid for the renovation and hired Angie's crew to do the work."

Cole let out a whistle. "Now that I've seen that renovation, I have a fair idea what it's worth. You deserve some free books. Maybe free books for life."

"Nah. One time is plenty. Doing something Dad would have loved means a lot to all of us. We're grateful to them, too. It's win-win."

"Alrighty, then." Cole opened his door. "Let's go fetch those books."

"Let's do." Jordan piled out with the rest of them, her anticipation building as they started walking toward the house. Her fingers itched to get hold of those books.

Luis lengthened his stride. "Guess we're race walking."

"Because I'm excited."

"Ever been to a book signing?"

"Nope. You?"

"This is my first."

"Mine, too." Cole came up on her other side. "I'm gonna start with Rance. Who's with me?"

"Me." Rio moved up, too, falling into step with Luis. "Hey, look at us, striding along with purpose, like we're heading for the OK Corral."

That made her laugh. "I'll be Wyatt. He was the cutest."

"You're thinking of Kevin Costner, sis."

"No, I looked up his actual picture and he was hot."

"If you say so. I see Morgan as more your type. Then are we all heading for Rance's line?"

"I'm fine with that." Luis looked over at her. "You in?"

She shook her head. "I'm starting with Oksana."

"Oh, then maybe I'll—"

"You don't need to come with me. Her line's shorter so I won't be long. I'll catch up with you guys."

"What if I want to come with you? I'll grab one of her books from the kitchen. Wouldn't hurt for me to learn something about what's it's like to be a miserable tween girl."

Cole chuckled. "You're showing your hand, Bridger."

<u>29</u>

Luis decided to play along with Cole's comment. "Might as well show my cards. She's already seen 'em."

"We all have," Rio said. "We're just waiting for Jordan to play hers."

"Oh, good grief." Jordan rolled her eyes. "I don't have any cards. Enough with the poker metaphors."

"Aw, c'mon." Cole put his arm around her and gave her a sideways hug. "The moment was begging for a poker metaphor. Especially since you wanna be Wyatt, who was a card shark. And by the way, Luis, don't ever play poker with this woman. She'll fudging clean you out."

"I believe you."

"Hey, Cole." Rio glanced down their four-person line. "Is it a coincidence that you say fudging a lot and Jordan's horse is named Fudge?"

"No, it is not. I'll tell you the story while we're in line to get Rance's autograph."

"Deal."

The conversation ended when they switched to walking single-file up the steps past lines for Desiree and Rance. Luis led the way to the kitchen.

The boxes in the pantry were already open and partly depleted. He quickly passed out books and the foursome split up.

The tables for Desiree and Rance were set up in the large room to the left of the front doors. Oksana was in the smaller one on the right.

After they got in the back of the line, Jordan glanced around. "This room's all non-fiction?"

"Right. Fiction is in the larger room across the hall. This used to be my great-grandmother's parlor."

"It still has that feel, with the antique chairs and lamps. It's perfect for Oksana's signing. More intimate."

"By Christmas it'll be even cozier. Angie's crew will create a coffee shop in the room on the other side of that wall. I think they're putting in an arched doorway to connect with this room."

"I can picture this house decorated for Christmas. It'll be gorgeous."

"It always was." Would she come back for the holidays? Would she wait that long?

Oksana's line was modest compared to Desiree's and Rance's, but she still had about thirty people. As he'd expected, he was the only guy.

The rest were an even mix of women and young girls with many mother-daughter combos in line together. He recognized a few but didn't know any of them well.

They acknowledged him with a nod followed by an amused smile when they caught sight of Oksana's book in his stack. He was clearly an outlier.

"Your reputation will never be the same," Jordan murmured. "You might have to turn in your man card."

"I don't know about that. I'm standing here with a hot woman who clearly enjoys my company. I'd say my rep's in fine shape."

That earned him a grin. "Thank you. That was nice." She took a breath. "What do you think of Cole?"

"I like him."

"He's never been without a job, at least in my memory. The minute he had any skills he was canvassing the neighborhood offering to cut lawns, wash cars, walk dogs, whatever people were willing to pay him for."

"Are you worried about him? You looked kind of unsettled when he made that announcement."

"I was. It's not like him to quit work without having any idea what he wants to do next."

"People change."

"He doesn't. Or he didn't."

"My dad used to say you couldn't grow without it."

"And we all miss him like crazy, don't we, Marv?"

"Harry and Marv?" Jordan spun around. "Oh, my goodness. I finally get to see you guys!"

"You know them?" Luis turned to face what everyone called the barber twins. They weren't related, but they had a similar chunky build and identical handlebar mustaches. And now he wasn't the only man in the room.

"These guys were kind enough to make room on the sidewalk so I had a place to stand and watch the parade," Jordan said. "How long have you been behind us? I thought we were the end of the line."

"We've been here a while." Marv's eyes had a suspicious twinkle.

Luis had seen that twinkle before. Marv was up to something. "You sure were quiet."

"That was on purpose." Harry gave Marv a look. "*He* was eavesdropping."

"I was and I make no apology for it. I have a horse in this race and I'm collecting evidence—"

"A horse in what race? What evidence?" Was the guy losing it?

"Okay, a horse race is the wrong analogy. I have a personal record to uphold, one I've maintained for... how long has it been, Harry?"

"You told me twenty-six years."

"Then let's say twenty-six years. Close enough. I'd hate to see it broken. For my sake, obviously, but mostly for yours and Jordan's."

Luis glanced at her. "Do you know what he's talking about?"

"I do." Her cheeks turned pink. "During the parade, when you and I caught sight of each other... I don't know if you remember, but—"

"I remember." Did he ever. Looking into her blue eyes again had been a gut punch he still hadn't recovered from.

"When Marv found out I knew you, he had a premonition about the two of us. I assured him he's very much mistaken."

"But am I?" Marv gazed at her with a knowing smile. "My sources tell me you've moved out to the ranch. Close proximity."

Luis got it now. "You think we'll end up together."

"Bingo. And you will, judging from the way you look at each other. Reminds me of Robert Redford and Meryl Streep in *Out of Africa*."

"Never saw it." Somehow he'd missed hearing about Marv's premonitions even though he'd been going in for haircuts since he was four.

"Don't bother watching the movie. Spend your time on the real thing. What you two have is built to last. And I'm never wrong, am I, Harry?"

"Not so far, but there's always a first time."

"And this is that first time, Marv." Jordan put a hand on the barber's shoulder. "Brace yourself. That squiggle you felt in your tummy yesterday morning was just something you ate for breakfast that didn't agree with you."

Clearly Jordan wasn't buying what Marv was selling. But he was. Not that it mattered if he believed they were fated to be together. If she thought it was superstitious nonsense, he was dead in the water.

Marv maintained his sunny smile. "We'll see, won't we? Hey, we're almost to the head of the line. How about that? Time flies when romance is in the air."

"You two are here to get a book signed?" He'd assumed they'd come in so Marv could check on his current fated couple project.

"Of course." Harry held up Oksana's book. "We read her first one the minute it came out. Can't wait to read the second one. We've already been through Rance's and M.R. Morrison's lines. Today's like Christmas for us."

Marv gave Luis's stack an approving glance. "I see you have all three, as well. Good job."

"Thanks." He turned toward the signing table just as the mom and daughter ahead of them walked away.

"Luis and Jordan." Oksana greeted them with a warm smile as they stepped up. "Are congratulations in order? Or are you two caught in the cross-fire?"

"It's more of a cross-fire situation." Jordan laid down her book. "I'm thrilled to be here, though, and get this one signed. I love Odette."

"Me, too." Pulling the book toward her, Oksana opened it and began to write. "For what it's worth, I can relate to your situation. Relationships are complicated enough as it is. Add in a big family, and things get ten times crazier." She closed the book and handed it back.

"No kidding. Thank you so much for signing this for me. It's great meeting you."

"Same here. Let me know how you like it."

"I will, for sure. Your turn, Luis."

Oksana's eyes widened as he put his copy on the table. "You're getting my book, too?"

"Lucky highly recommended it."

"Then I'm guessing you haven't read the first one."

"No, but I'll get it and read it before I read this one." Seemed like the right course of action.

"This one will make more sense if you do that." She broke eye contact and picked up her pen. "I'll be sure and thank Lucky for giving me a plug. And thank you, too, for trusting his judgment." She chuckled. "You do realize he's a mite prejudiced." She looked up and handed him the book.

"Maybe, but you should have heard his voice when he said you're a great writer. There was a ton of respect tucked into those words."

She flushed. "And that's why I love that cowboy. Thank you for telling me."

"Thank you for teaching about how young girls think."

She laughed. "You bet."

"Harry and Marv, she's all yours." He stepped aside to make room for the barber twins. Tipping his hat to them, he followed Jordan into the hallway.

She paused. "Hang on. I want to see what she wrote."

"She didn't just sign her name? I thought that's all she was supposed to do."

"That's all I expected, too, but she wrote something more. I couldn't see what it was." She opened to the title page. "Huh."

"What'd she say?"

"I hope you find your HEA."

"What's an HEA?"

"Happily-ever-after."

"Oh." He opened his book and flipped to the title page.

"What'd she put in yours?"

He stared at the message. "Same thing." Until this moment, he hadn't been clear on what he was going for with Jordan. But thanks to Oksana, he had a name for his ultimate goal. He wanted a fudging HEA.

<u>30</u>

"Rance and Desiree's lines are shorter than they were." Jordan pulled her phone out of her backpack and checked the time as she walked back down the steps with Luis.

"Considerably shorter. Have you seen Cole and Rio?"

"I haven't. They must be inside getting Rance's book signed." She stood behind the last people in Rance's line, a couple wearing shorts, tank tops and running shoes. Tanned and fit, they looked like they belonged on a California beach.

"You made the right call, choosing to go see Oksana first. We got to be inside where it's cool." He unsnapped the sleeves of his western shirt and rolled back the cuffs. "It's warm out here."

The simple move intended to cool him off had the opposite effect on her. Sunlight gleamed on his muscled forearms, highlighting a sprinkling of dark hair. Last night he'd braced himself on his forearms while he'd…. *whoa, easy, girl! Rein it in!*

"Jordan? You okay?"

She took a deep breath to calm herself. Didn't work. This close, she inhaled a heady dose of his aftershave mingled with the tempting aroma of his sun-warmed skin. She wanted to lick his arm. *Think about something else, doofus!*

"You're flushed. Why don't you go stand in the shade for a while? I'll hold your place."

"I'm… I'm okay."

"Are you sure? You might be dehydrated. I'm sure they have water inside. I'll go—"

"Never mind." She gripped his arm to stop him from leaving. Yep, still wanted to lick it and then move on to the part of his throat exposed by his open collar. "I'll be fine."

"Heat stroke is real, you know. I'll bet you are dehydrated. It can sneak up on you in the summer when—"

"Shh." She turned her back on the couple ahead of them. "Lean down," she murmured. "I don't want the whole world to hear this."

Giving her a puzzled glance, he hunched over.

Putting her mouth close to his ear, she resisted the urge to nibble on it while she explained what had set her off.

His cheek dented in a smile. "I'll be damned." Then he straightened and gazed at her, his dark eyes shining. "You know that makes me feel like a stud, right?"

"Evidently that's exactly what you are. I just suddenly… whoosh. I've been playing it cool all day, but when you did that, I came apart at the seams."

"Want me to roll 'em back down?"

"That would be stupid. To be clear, I've been around plenty of guys who did the same thing and I didn't come unglued."

"You're so good for my ego. Keep it up and before you know it, I'll be impossible to live with."

"You said that on purpose."

"Yes, I did."

"You don't believe me." Now that they were talking, she was in better control of herself.

"No, I don't."

"Will you believe Cole if he tells you?"

"I don't expect to hear that from Cole."

"I guess we'll see, won't we?"

"You sound like Marv."

"Ah, Marv. Sorry about those two."

"The barber twins? They're a fixture in Mustang Valley. Everybody gets a kick out of them."

"The barber twins, huh?" She chuckled. "I get a kick out of them, too. I just wish Marv would give up on this premonition thing."

"Have you considered that he could be right?"

Her breath caught. "No." She hesitated. Heck, might as well ask. "Have you?"

"Sure. I come from a culture that believes in destiny and the hand of Fate. What if we were supposed to meet five years ago, and now we're getting a second chance at happiness?"

"Fate didn't bring me here. I brought me here."

"Because of a dream."

"One that was driving me nuts. I was looking for the antidote."

"How's that working out for you?" He folded his arms over his chest and grinned, the rat.

"Not so great, smarty-pants. But I'm not blaming Fate or destiny for that."

"What are you blaming?"

She lowered her voice. "You're just too fudging hot."

"Backatcha." Then his attention shifted. "Here come Cole and Rio." He lifted a hand. "Over here!"

"Saw you!" Cole called out. "Will you look at this short line? We should've gone over to the Raccoon for a cool one and come back now."

"Yeah," Rio said, "but we'd better get in Desiree's line instead of gabbing. More people could show up any minute."

"Chances are they won't." Luis scanned the area. "I think the rush is over. Go ahead and stand over there just to be safe, but I'll bet you'll still be the end of the line when we come out."

Cole looked around, too. "You could be right. That'll make it easier if we end up going to her table together. Then we can head straight over to the Raccoon to meet up with Mila."

Jordan gave him a look and a shake of her head.

"I mean, or not. I guess that was supposed to be later. Never mind."

Rio tipped back his hat. "What's up with Mila?"

"It's just a discussion," Luis said. "The four of us need to... hash out a few things."

"So I'm not invited?" The sparkle left his eyes.

Jordan couldn't stand it. "Yes, you are." She'd become fond of this guy. Shutting him out of their talk would be an icky way to end the day. "But considering the topic, I wanted to have the same number of women as men, so—"

"You need Claudie, then. I'll get her." Rio took out his phone. "She's good at hashing things out. What time?"

"Let's say three-fifteen."

"Got it." He sent the text and seconds later his phone chimed with a reply. "She'll be there. What's the topic?"

"Luis and me."

"Hot damn. I have *so* much to say about that."

"Well, let's go stand in Desiree's line," Cole said, "and you can tell me some of those things while we're waiting. We can do a little pre-discussion brainstorming."

"Sounds like a plan."

As Cole passed by her, he leaned in close. "Thanks for saving my sorry ass."

"No worries. This might be better, anyway."

After they left, Luis stood looking at her, his hands in his pockets.

"What?"

"I know why you included Rio, which was kind of you. It's also logical to bring in another one of my sisters, but why would having more people in my family make it better? That's four Bridgers and two Sterlings. Not very balanced."

"I'm more interested in balancing the male viewpoint with the female one than the number of family members. Having more members of your family doesn't bother me. In fact, I like it."

"Why?"

"Because I do want to keep in touch with them. I'm hoping that they'll want to keep in touch with me even if you and I aren't together. The more they know about me and the reasons behind my choices, the better."

"I can't argue with that. I want to know all about you."

"Then it's a good thing my brother showed up, because nobody knows me better than he does."

"And vice-versa?"

"If you'd asked me yesterday, I would have said yes. But something's going on with him and I don't know what he's thinking."

"Is it possible something's going on with you and he wouldn't know what you're thinking?"

"I doubt it. I'm still the same person I was the last time we got together."

"No, you're not."

"How can you say that?"

"Because you're not the same person you were yesterday."

She had no comeback. He was right.

"Neither am I, *querida*," he said softly. "Neither am I."

31

They'd finally made it inside the large fiction room created by knocking down the wall that used to separate two smaller rooms. Rance's table was near the front window and Desiree's was in the back. Her line of fans hid her from view but Andy was visible at his post nearby.

Rance was easier to see. He also reminded Luis of someone. As he watched Rance kid around while he signed books, his behavior was somehow familiar. Yet this was the first time he'd met the guy.

Jordan turned to him. "Did you run into Beau McLintock this morning in the tunnel room?"

"Yeah, I certainly did, and... wait, that's it! I was trying to think who Rance reminds me of and it's Beau. They don't really look that much alike, but the way they talk, their mannerisms...."

"Makes sense. Beau is Rance's big brother. Rance probably idolized him the same way Rio idolizes you. He copied Beau's style and it's stuck with him."

"Rio doesn't idolize me."

"Wanna bet? He wants to learn to waltz so he can dance like you. He was the one bragging about your pitching in the state championship games. He got out of bed at five this morning because you were the one asking him to. I doubt he'd do that for Monty or Zay, at least not without a lot of grumbling."

He rubbed the back of his neck and sighed. "Auntie Kat said he idolizes me. I thought it was her way of buttering me up so I'd comply with her wishes."

"Both things could be true. It's obvious to me you're his role model."

"Auntie Kat said pretty much the same thing, that I could do for him what Dad did for me. But damn, that's a hell of a responsibility."

"Don't worry. You're up to it."

"You never met my dad. He left big boots to fill. He had a way about him. So much charisma."

"I didn't meet him, but I've met you. You have a way about you, too, Luis Bridger. And you're loaded with charisma. Trust me, I know how special you are. I've been around. Rio's in good hands."

Her speech made his face heat. "Thank you." It also raised a question. "If I'm all that and a bag of chips, why are you running away?"

"You know why. I love my work and I'm constantly on the go. That wouldn't make for—"

"We could work around travel plans."

"We're not a good match. I'm not right for you."

"I disagree."

"Look, this is why I took Cole's suggestion that we talk it out over a beer. He'll give you a different perspective. Let's not get into it now."

He did his best to tamp down his frustration. "I'm just confused. We have fun, you think I'm great, but you—"

"You know that old line? *It's not you, it's me*?"

"Yes, and it's a damn cop-out."

"Not always. In this case, it's the absolute truth."

"Only because you think—"

"Luis." She held up her hand.

He blew out a breath. She was right. This wasn't the place. But he was so ready to get everything out in the open.

She expected Cole to confirm she had issues, but admitting it didn't mean the situation was hopeless. People could overcome old conditioning if they had a reason to. They could compromise on the amount of time she spent on the road.

Since talking about it was a bad idea and he couldn't think about anything else, they waited in silence while the tanned couple in front of them laughed and chatted with Rance. Then it was their turn.

Jordan laid her book down. "Hi, I'm Jordan."

"Nice to meet you, Jordan."

"Congratulations on your first book."

"Thank you. They say it's like having a baby." He opened the book and started writing.

"I suppose it is."

He chuckled. "It's *nothing* like having a baby. No poopy diapers, no strained carrots on my shirt, no college fund to open." He handed back her book. "And I can give birth to as many as I want without worrying about overpopulation."

"Then I hope you have a fertile imagination like your mom."

"It was her gift to me. Have fun with the book."

"Thanks. I'm sure I will." She stepped away to make room for Luis.

He handed over his book. "My name's Luis. I'm—"

"Luis Bridger. Beau mentioned you."

"The tunnel?"

"Yeah." He grinned. "Said you took it like a man."

"More like a worm."

"I heard that, too. Now I'm putting it together. You two are the ones Granny said would be making wedding plans on the sly this afternoon."

"We're doing *what*?" He shot Jordan a look.

"I meant to tell you—"

"Yikes." Rance's eyes widened. "You don't know why you're meeting at the Raccoon? I'm so sorry, dude. I kinda think you're getting married really soon. Hope that doesn't come as a shock."

Jordan was pink with embarrassment. He couldn't picture her playing a joke on him. Not about this. Granny had misunderstood. But arguing the point with Rance, who adored Granny so much he'd put her in his book, wasn't a great idea, either.

He cleared his throat and managed a smile. "You know how it is. The groom's the last to know."

"Attaboy. Roll with the punches. I'm sure you two will be blissfully happy." He signed Luis's book and returned it. "Beau's looking forward to seeing you work with those wild horses."

"I'll be glad to have him. Good thing he said something. You kind of remind me of him. Not in looks, but...."

"It's no mystery. He was my role model from the time I could walk. Followed him everywhere. Whatever Beau did, I wanted to do."

"And now?"

"I'm his role model. He follows me everywhere. If I hadn't told him no, he'd be here right now." Then he laughed. "Nah, I still idolize the guy. I want to be him when I grow up. You two take care."

"We will." He put an arm around Jordan's shoulders as they walked into the hall. "Before we go back out, we need to—"

"She was lip-reading when I talked to Mila during lunch. Then she called me over to say she knew we'd be working out wedding details since the four people involved were you, me, my brother and your sister. She refused to believe that wasn't the purpose of our meeting, so I gave up."

He turned her to face him. "Well, that settles that. We'll have to get married."

Her eyes widened. "Are you nuts?"

"I'm kidding."

"Whew. You scared me for a second."

"Sort of. It's a great idea."

"No, it's not."

He opened his book to the title page. "Rance thinks it is." He showed her the page where Rance had written *Wishing you and Jordan a happy life together.*

"Oh, no. He ruined your book. You won't want to keep it now."

"Ah, but I do want to keep it. It doesn't wish us a happy marriage. Maybe we'll become besties."

32

"Maybe I should skip getting my M.R. Morrison book signed." Jordan descended the steps with Luis. Sure enough, Rio and Cole were still the last ones in Desiree's line.

"I'd hate for you to do that."

"I'd hate to do it, too, but I don't want—"

"Hey, guys!" Rio called out. "How'd you like Rance? He's a funny guy."

She sighed. "Yeah, he's a riot."

"What's wrong?" Cole stepped out of line and started toward her.

She motioned them to move away from the people ahead of them and lowered her voice. "Granny got the idea in her head that Luis and I are getting married and she told Rance."

"Oh, boy." Cole sucked in a breath.

"Luis didn't want to contradict Granny's story, so now Rance believes it and might even have told his mom."

"Or not," Luis said. "They've both been busy autographing books all afternoon."

"Or maybe Granny told Rance and his mom at the same time. I don't want to take that chance. I'm thinking I just won't get an autograph."

"No, no, we're not going that route, sis. You've loved those Morrison books ever since I can remember. You've collected every last one."

"Yeah, and they're all in your apartment! I didn't think of that. If you move out—"

"That's not a done deal. Even if I do leave, your books aren't a problem. I'll move them along with my stuff."

"The books aren't the only thing. There's the koala bear and the kangaroo. And my softball bat. And my glove—"

"Let's not worry about that now. We need to handle this little hiccup."

"It's not so little. Poor Luis has an autographed book but he'll have to rip out that page."

"No, I won't. I—"

"I guess you could put stickers over part of it. Show them what Rance wrote."

Setting Rance's book on top of his stack, he opened it to the title page. Both Cole and Rio came over to look.

"Fudge it all." Cole shook his head. "How did Granny get that idea into her head?"

"Remember at lunch when I went over to ask Mila to meet us at the Raccoon this afternoon? Granny was lip-reading and jumped to the conclusion the four of us were making wedding plans."

"How do you know?"

"She called me over and whispered it to me. I tried to tell her she was mistaken but she was convinced I was just trying to keep it a secret. I finally gave up."

"I can see how she might think that," Rio said.

"Me, too. Especially when I'm setting up a meeting with my brother and Luis's oldest sister. Logically that's the core of our wedding party."

Cole tugged down the brim of his hat. "Here's what we'll do. Since we'll be the last four in Morrison's line, we'll go up to the table as a group. Before she has a chance to say anything, one of us, probably Luis, will tell her there's this hilarious rumor going around that you two are getting married and it's simply not true."

Rio nodded. "That's good, especially the hilarious part. We can say it started as a crazy joke."

"Right." Cole glanced at Luis. "What else you say is up to you, but you need to be laughing like you find this hysterical. You're not upset. Neither of you can look upset. That's the key. My guess is she'll follow your lead and laugh with you. Bottom line, she won't write some BS in your book or Jordie's."

"It's worth a shot, and I don't have any better ideas."

"Me, either. Good thinking, big brother. Maybe if we convince her, she'll pass the word to the rest of the family." She turned to Luis. "But I'm sorry about your book."

"I'm not. Think of it this way. It'll make a good story."

"Speak for yourself. This isn't one I'll be telling around the campfire."

"You never know, sis. Given enough time, you just might." Cole checked out the line. "Hey, we'd better catch up. They're at the top of the steps already."

She and Luis got back in line behind Cole and Rio.

"A softball bat, huh?" Luis gazed at her with a soft glow in his eyes.

"Uh-huh." Obviously he wasn't upset about his ruined book. She still was. Could she have prevented it by speaking up? Just as she'd feared, she was causing him problems.

"Jordie was a star," Cole said over his shoulder. "She had a change-up nobody could hit."

"Interesting. That was my go-to pitch. How long did you play?"

"All four years."

"Went to State twice." Cole turned back to face them. "Coulda had a scholarship but by then she'd read Buck Brannaman and was hooked."

"Luis went to State twice." Rio turned around, too. You guys are like twinsies. Now I'm starting to wonder why you don't get married. Maybe Granny's onto something."

Luis gave him a look. "Watch it, little brother."

"Just sayin'." He grinned.

Their teasing made her stomach churn, especially because there was an underlying message there. Everyone but her thought this matchup was a darned good idea.

Well, not everyone. Cole still hadn't weighed in. Being friendly with Luis wasn't the same as giving his blessing. Her big brother would never be quick to do that.

"Hey, the line's inside the building." Luis tugged on the brim of his hat. "*Andale, muchacos.*"

"All you need is a mask and a cape, Bridger."

Rio laughed. "I know, right? You should have seen the way he dipped Jordan at the end of their waltz last night. Totally Zorro."

"You waltz?" Cole sounded impressed. "Bet you loved that, sis."

"It was fun." Fun didn't even begin to describe that dance. She was glad Cole hadn't been there to see it.

The four of them walked into the fiction room of the bookstore. Rance's table was empty, that part of the signing over.

They followed the last few in Desiree's line to the back of the room. Soon two older women who looked like they might be sisters were the only ones ahead of them.

Now that only a few people were in the room, Jordan was struck by the quiet majesty of the space. With its high ceilings, and multipaned windows, it looked like the library of an elegant home. Beautifully finished shelves and stained-glass chandeliers made her catch her breath.

This venue would become famous. The world hadn't discovered it yet, but word would spread. Someday it might be hard to get in. This signing with M.R. Morrison was history in the making.

How lucky she was to be here in this moment, about to have her book signed by the author who would be eternally connected to the bookstore's opening day. She snuck a peek at Luis and discovered he was watching her. "Luis, this place...."

"I know. I feel it, too. Like the beginning of something very special."

"Yeah."

The ladies ahead of them picked up their books and walked away, leaving only the four of them facing a smiling and somewhat weary Desiree and Andy. As if they'd planned it, they fanned out.

Desiree laughed. "Looks like the Earp brothers and Doc Holliday have arrived."

"Yay, she thinks like me!" Rio grinned. "I said the same thing a while ago." He tipped his hat. "I'm Rio. Should we call you Ms. Morrison? I never asked anybody about that."

"You should call me Desiree. The Bridger Bunch is family, now."

"Speaking of family." Luis stepped forward. "I'm Luis, by the way. I don't know if you remember—"

"Oh, I remember you, Luis. You're the horse whisperer. You'll be showing up in one of my books someday. You'll be one of the good guys."

He flushed. "Thank you. That would be an honor."

"I take it you'd like me to sign your book."

"Yes, ma'am, but first I have something funny to tell you. There's a wild rumor going around that—"

"You and Jordan are getting married. I know. I've heard it. Please don't tell Granny I said this, but she's an unreliable narrator."

"You don't believe her?"

"Sure don't. Your mom said Jordan's only been in town since Thursday night. I've come to know your character through Mila's diaries on the H&H website. Jumping into marriage after a couple of days doesn't fit at all."

A weight slipped off Jordan's shoulders. She should have trusted this woman to question Granny's story. She hadn't gotten where she was by being gullible.

"No, it doesn't," Luis said, "but I guess Rance hasn't been reading the diaries because he was ready to believe."

"Rance adores Granny and sometimes he lets that get in the way of his better judgment. That sweet lady's a born romantic and so is my youngest son, for that matter. Something dramatic like a wedding following a whirlwind courtship would appeal to both of them They'd want it to be true."

"So they'll be disappointed."

"They'll get over it. That's the other side of being susceptible to a fantasy. If one doesn't pan out, another one might." She shifted her attention to Jordan. "I'm sorry if this caused you grief."

"I mostly was sad about the book Rance signed for Luis. He wrote that he wished us a happy life together."

Desiree held her gaze. "But that doesn't mention an impending wedding."

"I guess not, but it still implies one will take place."

"And it won't? Not ever?"

She said *no* at the same time Luis said *the jury's still out.* She sent him a look.

He shrugged. "That's my opinion."

Desiree smiled and glanced over at Andy, who stood with his hands in his pockets. "Does this sound familiar?"

"Yes, ma'am." He gazed at Luis. "I've been where you are, son. Be patient. Sometimes a miracle happens."

"That would be nice, sir."

"Call me Andy. I have a feeling we're going to be good friends."

"Wait." Jordan stared at Desiree. "He wanted to marry you and you said no?"

"I certainly did."

"But why?"

"Because I thought I was too strong and set in my ways for marriage, especially when I was about to turn sixty. That was my cover story, anyway. Underneath that belief I was scared to death."

She hugged her stack of books and tried to stop shaking. "Of what?"

"Taking down the walls. Letting him in."

"B-but you must have. You married him."

"I did."

"They weren't all down," Andy said. "I had to climb through a window."

That made Cole laugh. "You're my kind of guy, Andy. If you make friends with Luis, I'd like to tag along."

"Glad to have you, whoever you are."

"Cole Sterling, Jordan's brother."

"Pleased to meet you, Cole Sterling. I'd welcome you to town but it's not my town. Hey, is anybody interested in having Dez sign a book? I think she might have four more autographs left in her."

Jordan took a breath. "I am." She stepped forward and laid down *The Wayward Rider.* "Like I said when we met at the Raccoon, I've been reading you forever. I have every book you've ever written."

"Even the *Ranch Puppy* series?"

"Those, too. I'm saving them for my—" She caught herself. She'd never spoken that out loud and didn't want to now, of all times. "For my brother's kids, if he ever gets around to having them."

"I'll be putting out more, maybe even throw in a *Ranch Kitty* story. My grandkids made me promise." She finished writing, closed the book and slid it across the table. Then she leaned closer. "Try not to be scared," she murmured. "It wastes time and time is precious."

Jordan soaked up the kindness in Desiree's voice. "Yes, ma'am." Taking the book, she turned around. And there was Luis, his brown eyes filled with tenderness and love.

Taking a breath, she walked away from the table and into a corner set up as a reading nook with a chair and lamp. She opened the book. What deep words of wisdom would she find?

Good grief. Desiree had written a fudging essay.

To Jordan—I promise you're safe with this Bridger Bunch. As for Luis... you can always tell a man's character by how he treats his horse. I didn't have that yardstick for Andy. He didn't have a horse. I had to take my chances and it's worked out. You're in luck, though. Luis is wonderful with horses, even wild ones. It's a good sign. Wishing you happiness, Desiree, aka M.R. Morrison

33

Cole offered Rio a lift over to the Raccoon, leaving Luis and Jordan alone for the first time since they'd left the ranch. He should make use of the opportunity to say something significant, words that would open that window Andy had mentioned.

But his brain was like the traffic in Missoula at rush hour. What he needed was a long ride on Scout so he could sort through all the thoughts swirling in his head. That wouldn't be happening today.

He made a guess that Jordan was in the same fix, maybe even thinking how nice a ride on Fudge would be right now. He had evidence. She was on her phone and a glance at her screen told him Monty had sent her some shots of Fudge in his stall.

"How's he doing?"

"Good. Real good. Monty's happy with his progress. He and Zay caught a ride back in your mom's van, so he'll be checking on Fudge in person soon."

"I didn't think about the fact that Mila and Claudie might need a ride over." Showed how distracted he'd been.

"I texted them to ask about that. Your mom just dropped them off at the Raccoon. They're getting us a table for six."

"If I'd thought of it, we could have brought them over."

"I think they wanted to give us a chance to be alone."

"Ah. I guess Mila and Claudie will ride back with us."

"Maybe. But they're both curious about my brother. They've seen him but haven't had a chance to actually talk to him so they might decide to ride back in his truck."

"Does he have room? What does he drive?"

"A truck like mine. He has a regular backseat. Remember his remark about the shotgun?"

"Does he really keep one there?"

"He doesn't even own one."

"Good thing he was kidding about it. That wouldn't go over well with Mila and Claudie. Or Monty. We've taken in way too many horses with gunshot wounds."

"The only thing Cole likes to shoot is pool."

"Then he needs to know there's a table in the house."

"There is?"

"You play?"

"When I get a chance. It's a great game."

"Then we should find time for it while you're here." So she played pool, too. Every conversation turned up another point of connection. Was she seeing what he was seeing?

"If we can. Maybe tomorrow. The past two days have been...."

"Intense."

"To put it mildly."

"Well now you can relax with a beer and some good conversation." The street on the Raccoon's side of the square was no longer blocked off and all the tables and chairs were gone. Two parking spots were available right in front of the Raccoon.

"Very funny."

"You don't have to do this." Taking the space nearest the door, he shut off the engine and turned toward her. "It's totally voluntary."

She met his gaze. "Backatcha. It was Cole's idea. You don't have to go along."

"But I want to. He's known you all your life. He's stuffed with info and I want to hear what he has to say."

"It'll be good for you to get his perspective. I warn you it won't be all sunshine and roses."

"That's fine."

"I thought it might be complicated with him here this weekend, but I'm glad he showed up."

He smiled. "Almost feels like he was supposed to."

Amusement glimmered in her eyes. "You and Marv." Then her attention shifted. "There's Cole's truck."

He looked over at a pickup that was exactly like hers. "Did you buy the same truck?"

"He got his first and made a joke about Sterling silver. When I could afford it, I got the same thing and used the association as my brand."

"Smart." He reached for his door handle. "Let's do this."

The four of them met on the sidewalk and Rio grinned. "It's the OK Corral all over again."

"Too bad we can't get through the door that way." Cole gestured toward Jordan. "Ladies first."

Her backpack over her shoulder, she led them in. Luis stood back and motioned for Cole to follow her. Time to get a little distance and become more observer than participant.

After going through the door, Cole paused and gazed at the raccoon trio over the bar. "I noticed that at lunch. Great decoration."

The comment surprised him until he remembered the raccoons hadn't performed during lunch.

Jordan turned around. "It's more than a decoration. It's animatronic."

"You mean like Disney animatronic?"

"Yep."

"Did they do something during lunch and I missed it?"

"No they didn't, now that you mention it. Luis, why didn't they perform?"

"I'm not sure." He looked to see if Clem was around and spotted him behind the bar. "Hey, Clem, is there a problem with the raccoons? Is that why you didn't turn them on during lunch?"

"No problem. I figured our visiting authors might want an oasis of calm while they ate."

"Any chance you'd be willing to show my friend what they can do?"

"Be glad to. It's way too quiet in here, anyway."

"Great call, bro." Rio stepped around him and addressed the scattering of customers. Mila and Claudie had secured a round six-top on the far side of the room, which was almost deserted. "Raccoon alert, folks! Get ready to sing!"

Cole grinned. "A sing-along? I love it."

"Here we go!" Clem flicked a switch behind the bar, the raccoons sprang to life and most of the small crowd started singing.

Rio and Luis joined in. So did Jordan, who'd heard the tune several times the night before.

We're rockin', yes we are, and hangin' in this bar, cause we are like family as you all can plainly see, so keep on rockin' tonight! We're rockin', yes we are, and drinkin' at this bar, come join us, near and far and keep on rockin' tonight!

Grinning like a little kid, Cole watched the raccoons. "That's awesome!" He looked over at Clem. "Would you be willing to play it one more time?"

"Why not?" Clem hit the switch again.

This time Cole joined in on the singing and managed well considering he'd only heard the lyrics once. When it was over, he turned back to Jordan. "Give me a minute with him, okay?"

"Sure."

Walking over to the bar, he shook hands with Clem. Then he started asking questions.

Jordan chuckled. "Did I mention that he's an electrician?"

"I heard construction," Luis said, "but no specifics."

"He can do all the things, but his passion is electricity and he's fascinated with animatronics. We should probably go sit down. He might be a while."

"Fine with me." Luis followed her.

"Yeah, I'm ready for a beer." Rio brought up the rear. "We can go ahead and order. I know what he wants. We talked about beer on the way over. Well, beer and women. We decided beer is way easier to understand."

Jordan laughed. "That sounds like my brother. He hasn't had the best luck finding the right person."

Luis filed away that tidbit, although Cole wasn't the only one with that problem. Finding the right person was tough. Even if you did they might not want you.

Mila gestured to the six water glasses. "We got this much started but decided not to order anything until you arrived."

"What's up with Cole?" Claudie glanced toward the bar.

"My brother's been fascinated with animatronics for years." Jordan took a seat next to Claudie. "We can order, though. Between Rio and me, we have a lock on what Cole wants."

"That's terrific," Mila said, "but everybody's on break except Clem. He's the one who brought us the water, so we'll have to... oh, never mind. They're coming over."

Luis made a command decision and walked around the table to sit next to Mila. Rio took the chair next to him, leaving the one beside Jordan for Cole. Perfect. He planned on doing a lot more listening than talking.

"Your brother's cute." Claudie lowered her voice but he still heard it, along with Jordan's quick *yes, he is.*

He'd been so focused on his own issues he hadn't considered that one of his sisters might show an interest in Cole. It would have been a nonstarter if Jordan's brother still had a job in Helena, but now….

Would this be a good thing or a bad thing? Either way it could be a very complicated thing. What else was new?

<u>34</u>

Jordan sipped on her beer and munched on pretzels and nuts, mostly because it gave her something to focus on other than Luis. The kitchen staff was also on a break, so they were limited to whatever was available at the bar.

At first the conversation was simple chitchat about the autograph party. Cole supplied a few basic facts about himself for Mila and Claudie's benefit.

Luis was mostly quiet, and Jordan couldn't shake the notion that he was in horse whisperer mode. Five years ago he'd described in detail how his dad had taught him to understand wild horses through quiet observation.

Luis's seating choice put him across the table from her. Was she the wild horse in this scenario?

Rio's comment about his conversation with Cole was a reminder that her brother had never had a serious relationship. She vaguely remembered him saying years ago that he wasn't sure marriage was for him. She'd dismissed it at the time, but maybe they were both destined to be single.

Cole nudged back his hat and cleared his throat, which always signaled he was ready to say his piece. She put down her beer and took a deep breath.

Leaning forward, he rested his arms on the table. "Since I suggested this gabfest, I'll start the ball rolling. We're here to discuss the relationship between my sis and Luis. I think it's great they're willing to let us help talk it through."

"So am I," Mila said. "I'm glad you suggested doing this."

"I didn't know I'd get so many of the Bridger Bunch involved, but the more the merrier. I've only caught a glimpse of what your family is all about, but I guaran-damn-tee you're nothing like the family Jordie and I were saddled with. You folks love and support one another. We didn't get that."

Mila, Claudie and Rio all flinched, but Mila was the one who spoke. "Was it physical abuse?"

"Just one time when my dad took a belt to me. But they didn't care enough to expend the energy it would take to beat us. They just made sure we felt like crap about ourselves."

Claudie swore under her breath.

"Now that we're older," Jordan said, "we know they did it because they felt like crap about themselves. Likely still do. But...."

"The damage was done." Claudie gave her a sideways hug. "I'm so sorry, Jordan. You, too, Cole."

"It is what it is," Cole said. "We've both struggled with it in our own way. I've pretended it didn't affect me, that I can build a life that works and be perfectly fine. Jordie will have to speak for herself on that."

"Same."

"The point is, when you believe you're unlovable, you don't let anyone get too close. I'm an expert at that. But my little sis, here, let this guy get under her skin." He looked at her. "Am I right?"

She nodded and avoided looking across the table. "Which is a problem because he's fallen for me and he deserves somebody better."

Luis exploded. "Don't say that! I promised myself I would just listen, but—"

"Easy, dude." Cole gave him a look. "I'm still debating whether you're good enough for *her*."

"What?" She stared at her brother. "Have you been paying attention? He's kind, considerate and funny. Any woman would be lucky to—"

"Any woman but you?"

"Yes! Because after all those years fighting with mom, that's my default. Luis hasn't seen it yet, but it would come out if we spent more time together. Mom was right. I'm impossible to live with. Tell them about those fights."

"The fights." His jaw tightened. "Screaming you could hear all around the neighborhood. It was the worst when Jordie had achieved something major and mom couldn't stand that. She'd criticize me, too, but Jordie got it worse. And she fought back."

"Good for you." Mila sent her a warm glance of support. "Never let the turkeys get you down."

"But Luis isn't a turkey," Rio said. "He wouldn't—"

"She doesn't trust him not to," Cole said.

"I wouldn't say that."

"What about your achievement with this clinic? Do you trust him not to undermine all your hard work?"

She opened her mouth but Luis got ahead of her.

"I admire the hell out of what you've done. You know I do."

"But what about the traveling, Bridger? Because clearly your life is here with the wild horses."

"I'm flexible. I figured she'd travel some, stay here some. I know she loves being on the road, so I wouldn't expect her to stay—"

"Hold it, *hermano*." Mila focused on him with the intensity of a laser. "Are you about to say you wouldn't *expect* her to stay home all the time? That you'd be okay if she left now and then?""

"Something like that."

"I'm not hearing flexibility. I'm hearing male privilege."

"No, it isn't. I—"

"Have you considered changing your life to suit hers?"

He looked confused. "I'm not sure what you mean."

"Couldn't you go on the road with her? Help her with her clinic?"

Jordan blinked. "I could never ask that of him. He loves it here. And he's the key to the rehabilitation program." She met his gaze across the table. "Seriously, don't even think about it."

"I'll admit I never have, but—"

"You shouldn't. Sorry, Mila. I appreciate your feedback, but that's crazy."

"No crazier than him asking you to curtail your travel because he intends to stay put. And let's not forget that Rio will start training next week to learn Luis's job."

"That's right, I will. And I'm a fast learner. Ask anybody."

Luis turned to him. "I believe you'll give it your all, but—"

"There's something else I've been meaning to say about the rehabilitation program." Mila glanced at her sister. "Is this a good time or a bad time?"

"A good time. The only reason we haven't talked to him is he's always so busy."

"Okay, then." She took a breath. "Ever since Dad died, you've worked yourself to the bone to keep adoptions at the same number they were when he was alive. It's lovely to adopt out horses, but financially you could cut back, especially now with the digital adoptions bringing in revenue."

"It's satisfying work."

"But he wouldn't want you to kill yourself doing it. And neither would the rest of us."

"I promise my job's not a burden."

"If you say so. But if you cut back, you'd have time to travel with Jordan, and you could be an ambassador for H&H along the way."

"She sounds like she doesn't want me to do it."

"I don't." A selfish part of her was picturing them on the road together. But it wouldn't be fair to him or the rehabilitation program.

"I love what I do, Mila."

"Unless I'm mistaken, you also love Jordan."

Cole leaned back, a smile on his face. "I like how this woman thinks." He surveyed the table. "Anybody have more to add?"

Nobody spoke.

"Then I guess we all have some cogitating to do."

Luis took a deep breath. "I do, for sure. Who's ready to head for home?"

"I am." Jordan stood, picked up her backpack and dug out her wallet. "What's the—"

"It's on me," Cole said. "Clem has my credit card and instructions to put everything on it."

"But you just quit your job."

"I quit my job, but I didn't say I was broke. I've been saving up. Must've known the day would come when I was ready to kick over the traces." He glanced at Luis, who had rounded the table. "Nice feeling. You should try it."

"Thanks, not for me. Anybody else need a ride back?"

"I think we're all set if Cole is willing to take us back," Mila said.

"Absolutely."

"Great. Thanks." Mila left her chair. "I'll just walk these guys out and be right back."

Once the three of them reached the sidewalk, she turned to Luis. "You are *mi corazon*, my heart, *hermano*. I didn't want to say this inside, but I think you're working like a maniac out of grief."

"No." His voice was soft. "No, I'm not."

"Okay, so you don't believe me, but it's true. And this woman is here to fill that hollow place in your heart." She glanced at Jordan. "And he can heal the hollow place in yours. You belong together, *hermanita*."

Her breath hitched. *Hermanita* meant little sister.

"That's all I have to say." Giving Luis a quick kiss on the cheek, she hugged Jordan and went back inside.

He gazed at her. "What do you think?"

"I can't think anymore."

"Me, either. I just need you."

"Same here."

"Let's go."

35

Silence filled the cab on the way home. The discussion Luis had hoped would bring clarity had only made everything more complicated. Mila thought he should throw his lot in with Jordan. But she didn't want him to.

Or did she? He'd seen something in her expression toward the end of the conversation that made him wonder. But what did he want?

Right now the answer was simple. He wanted to sink into Jordan's sweet body and forget about everything but loving her. That much was simple. It wouldn't solve anything, but it would temporarily blot out the confusion and replace it with happiness.

When he pulled up next to the casita, she was out before he was. "Is it locked?" she called out.

"No!" He barreled through the door she'd left open and slammed it shut. Following her trail of clothes, he ripped off his own, hopping on one foot as he yanked off each boot.

He was panting as he charged into the bedroom. It was still bright with sunlight. Unfastening his jeans and shoving them down along with his briefs, he devoured the sight of her flinging away her bra and kicking aside her panties.

His golden girl stood naked, her breasts quivering with each ragged breath. She crossed to the nightstand, opened the drawer and picked up a handful of condoms.

He laughed. "Really?"

"You never know." She threw one at him and tossed the rest on the nightstand. Then she got to work on the bed, flipping back the covers, pitching the pillows on the floor. Then she leaped onto the bed and lay flat, panting. "Hurry."

"Yes, ma'am." He fumbled with the condom and finally got the damn thing on. Climbing into bed, he positioned himself between her sleek thighs, made eye contact and thrust deep.

She clutched his ass. "I'm gonna come."

"Do it." He pumped hard and gritted his teeth as her cries and her spasms pushed him to the edge. By some miracle he held on and kept going.

She groaned. "Oh, Luis. *Luis.*" And she came again, harder this time.

He was a man possessed. So good, so damned good and he wasn't stopping. Not yet, even if he was gasping and shaking, even if his head was about to explode. "Once more."

He shifted the angle, watched the glow in her eyes, her parted lips as she sucked in one quick breath after another. "I love you." He gulped for air. "And you love me back."

"Yes."

"Say it." He stroked faster. "Say it, *querida.*"

"I love you." She arched into him. "I love you!"

He pushed deep and let go, the gush of his orgasm making him shudder and groan like a man in pain. But there was no pain, not in his body and not in his heart. Only joy.

Holding his position as long as he dared, he gazed into her eyes, so very blue. "Mila's right."

She gasped. "What?"

"Unless you don't want me there."

"At my clinics?"

"At your clinics, in your trailer, in your bed."

Her eyes narrowed. "It's the sex talking."

"No, it's me talking. We should do what Mila said. Unless you don't want me."

"I don't want you to give up work you love."

"I won't. I'll still do it sometimes. But mostly I'll—"

"Stop talking. This is only because we just had—"

"No, it isn't. But I have to get out of bed. I'll be right back." He headed for the bathroom. How had he been such an idiot? Mila was right about everything, even why he'd pushed himself so hard the past two years.

Jordan was here for a reason, to pry him away from his grief-driven, ego-driven mission to honor his father. And she needed him just as much as he needed her.

By going with her and teaming up for her clinics, he'd be constantly showing her she was fabulous instead of only speaking the words. He'd called himself flexible. He hadn't been, but he was now.

Toweling off, he called out to her. "Tell you what. You have a clinic next weekend, right?" He walked into the bedroom.

She was gone.

Cussing a blue streak, he pulled on his briefs and jeans, then his boots, no time for the socks.

She'd left the door open. Again. He hot-footed it outside, leaving the door ajar. He'd be back soon. With her.

He spotted her more than halfway to her trailer, running like hell. Shouting her name, he took off.

She didn't stop, didn't even slow down. If anything, she ran harder, head down, arms pumping.

He called out again, but she kept going. Damn, the woman was fast. Must've run track. He put on the afterburners, but she'd had a good head start.

Could he make it before she got to the trailer? He'd have blisters after this but who cared? Dammit, he was still a good five yards away when she reached the steps.

She didn't take time to look back. She just pounded up those steps, yanked open the door and jumped inside.

"Jordan!" As he reached for the door handle, a click told him she'd just locked it.

He banged on it, anyway. "Don't do this! It wasn't the sex talking!"

No answer.

"I love you! We belong together, *querida*!"

Still nothing.

"Look, I know you think I lost my mind just because we had good sex, but I didn't lose my mind, it cleared my mind. Open up! Please!"

"Hey there, bro."

He turned around. Sucked in air. "Hey, Monty." Had his brother seen the whole mad dash? Did he care? "What're you up to?"

"I just changed Fudge's bandage. I take it there's a wee problem, as Kieran would say?"

He took another shaky breath. "It's mostly my fault."

"Mostly?"

He grimaced. Reviewed his behavior. "All my fault. During the discussion at the Raccoon, Mila threw an idea at me I wasn't ready for, and I bobbled the ball."

Monty nudged back his hat. "But you must've recovered. I distinctly heard something about good sex in that rant of yours. So did Fudge, by the way. He sent me out here to get the 411."

"Sorry." He'd startled Jordan's injured horse with his shouting. Way to compound his mistakes. "How's he doing?"

"Better'n you."

"No kidding." He muttered a curse. "That's what I get for rushing."

"You proposed?"

"No, but..." He waved a hand. "Never mind the details. I knew she was skittish about Mila's plan. I *knew* it. But I could also see it was perfect. Like an idiot, I charged ahead."

"And she thinks sex is what changed your mind?"

"Yep. And she bolted."

"Is she right that it was the sex?"

"No! I mean sort of. But you know that moment of euphoria, when things become really clear?"

"I'm not sure I do. It's been a while."

"Well, I promise you that this was a breakthrough, not some reaction to endorphins."

"I'm willing to believe you, but I'm not the one you need to convince."

"I know. Guess I'll just stay put. Eventually she'll want to go see how Fudge is."

Monty looked him up and down. "You'll wait looking like that?"

"If I go home to change, she could slip out, check on Fudge and be back in her trailer before I can catch her."

"You are one lovesick puppy, bro."

"I am, but the good news is she loves me back."

"Are you sure? Because you standing out here half-naked and her inside with the door locked doesn't exactly telegraph Romeo and Juliet."

"I know, but—" Tires crunched on dirt. "Oh, hell. That's Cole's truck rolling in."

"Does *he* still like you?"

"I'm not sure."

"FYI, this scenario won't help your cause any."

"But if I try to dodge him, that'll look worse. Besides, he's staying in her trailer, so she'll have to open up when he arrives, right?"

"If you're counting on slipping past her big brother, your brain's more compromised than I thought."

"I'll just wait here and see how it works out."

Monty glanced at the trailer. "Just so you know, the side window is open a crack. I'm sure she's heard every word that's come out of your mouth."

"I don't care. I hope she did. I have nothing to hide."

"Well, I'll leave you to it. I'm heading up to the house. We'll all be having dinner before the Damsels claim Granny for the evening. If you get this worked out with Jordan, come join us."

"Will do." After Monty left, he watched as Cole dropped Mila and Claudie at the mini hacienda before driving up the hill to Rio's chalet. At last the truck came back down and headed for the trailer.

It slowed as it approached, as if Cole had finally noticed him standing there. Pulling up beside Jordan's truck, he shut off the engine and climbed out.

Luis shoved his hands in his pockets. "I know what this looks like."

"If you do, then please enlighten me, because I have no fudging idea what this looks like."

"Well, Jordan and I had some fun and games, and right afterward it was like a light went on in my brain. I knew Mila was right, so..." He paused, took a breath. "I told Jordan we should do what Mila said."

"Oh, boy."

"Yeah. She freaked out, ran to the trailer and locked herself in."

"She outran you?"

"She had a big head start."

"How could you possibly miss that she was on the run?"

"I was... um... cleaning up."

Cole scrubbed a hand over his face. Looked like he might've been covering up the fact he was laughing. "So now you want to travel with my sister and she doesn't want you to. Is that it?"

"She wants me to. She said she loves me, but she thinks I'll be unhappy if I cut way back on my work with the wild horses."

"Because you indicated that at the Raccoon."

"I know. Mila caught me by surprise. But I've seen the light."

"After you had some amazing sex?"

"Yes, but I swear it's not the sex talking, which is what she thinks. It just cleared out the cobwebs so I could see that Mila was right." He gazed at Cole. "That can happen sometimes."

"It can."

"Will you talk to her?"

"Not while you're standing out here. I suggest you go home, shower and shave. And wait."

"Do I have a choice?"

"Not really."

"Okay, then. She has my number if she wants to call or text me."

"She said she loves you? You're not making that up?"

"No."

"Then she'll be in touch."

"Thanks." He walked back to his casita. His future was in the hands of a man he'd met just hours ago. But Jordan trusted her brother. So would he.

<u>36</u>

"Jordie, it's me."

She blew her nose and tossed the tissue in the trash. "Is he out there?"

"No. I sent him back to his place."

She walked to the door and opened it.

Taking off his hat, Cole came in, filling the space the way Luis had. Tears threatened again and she grabbed another tissue from the box.

"Ah, Jordie. Don't cry." He hugged her close.

She lost it, soaking his shirt. "I d-don't cry."

"That's why I know this guy's important to you."

"I love him, damn it."

"He told me. He loves you, too."

"I know! That's the p-problem! He's gonna give up his beloved wild horse training for m-me."

"But what if that's what he needs to do?"

"How can it be? He loves it so much."

"It's not like he'll totally give it up. Mila didn't mean for him to do that. But he's been obsessing over it since his dad died. After you left she came back in and talked to us about what she said to him outside."

"I thought she didn't want you guys to know."

"She just didn't want to say it to him in front of everyone. She believes you two are meant for each other, that you were supposed to show up. He needed you."

She slowly extricated herself and blew her nose. "But he defended his job while we sat there at the Raccoon, then he changed his mind less than an hour later, right after we had great sex. How can I trust that?"

"What if I told you it's happened to me?"

"When?"

"Quite recently. It's why I quit my job."

"Are you involved with someone?"

"Not anymore."

Great. Now her brother wasn't making sense, either. "Come sit." She tugged him over to the bench. "Tell me."

"I was seeing someone. It wasn't a love match but the sex was good. Not like your deal, where you have good sex and love."

"You make it sound so simple. It's not. Anyway, go on."

"Last week we had this terrific time and ironically, right afterward I knew we had to break up and I had to quit my job. Neither one gave me what I really needed."

"Did you tell her while you were still in bed together?"

"Luis did that?"

"Yes."

Cole pressed his lips together, but he looked more amused than upset. "Well, we all make mistakes. I didn't do that, but I can see why he might get carried away. He knows you love him and he wants to close the deal. I was the opposite. I wanted to break up."

"Yeah, way different." She swallowed. "Are you saying that Luis's change of heart might be legit?"

"It might. Mila's bond with him is like yours and mine. She can tell he's in love with you and she thinks you're the best thing that could happen to him."

"What about you? What do you think?"

"I like the guy so far, but I just got here, sis. I like his family, too, what I've seen of them. Bottom line, I don't feel qualified to advise you."

She nodded. "That's fair."

"I told him you'd be in touch. He said you could call or text. But you don't have to rush into a decision one way or the other. We can both bunk in here. I'll take the foldout."

And he would, no matter how much she argued with him or how uncomfortable he'd be. She could hide out here with her big brother for as long as she needed to. "I'm so glad you're here."

"Me, too. Funny how things work out. It's almost like I was supposed to connect with you this weekend."

"Do you believe in this Fate stuff?"

"I didn't think I did. But after several months of not seeing you, here I am during a consequential time in your life."

"That's no mystery. You heard about the book signing and thought of me."

"That was totally random. I was eating lunch yesterday at a diner and a guy next to me was reading on his phone. Turned out to be one of Morrison's books and he told me about the autograph party."

"Huh." She took a deep breath and stood. "You know what? I need to discuss this matter with Fudge. He has a stake in it, too."

He smiled. "Good plan. While you're doing that, I'll fetch my books and my duffle from the truck."

After splashing cold water on her face and running a brush through her hair, she left the trailer and headed for the barn.

She caught Fudge dozing, but his head came up and his ears pricked forward the minute she called his name. He knickered softly.

"Same to you, sweet boy." She let herself into his stall and wrapped her arms around his neck. With a sigh, he laid his head on her shoulder, totally relaxed.

Her throat tightened. "You like it here, don't you, Fudgie?" It was something she'd noticed subconsciously but never acknowledged. She rested her cheek against his neck. "I like it here, too. Maybe too much. It scares me." She stroked his neck, her fingers moving in time with her thoughts. "You don't seem to have that problem. Ever since we got here, you've acted like you just assume everyone will love you."

She took his soft groan as agreement. "Whereas I worry that I'm... difficult."

He blew through his nostrils, which made her smile. "You sound like Luis. He doesn't believe it either." She slid her hand under his silky mane to give him a scratch. "But he does believe in Fate. Do you?"

No answer.

"Yeah, it's a puzzler. And now Cole sounds like he might put some stock in it." She absorbed the solid warmth of her horse, letting their deep connection soothe her.

"Cole says mom was critical of me 'cause she was jealous. One thing's for sure. Something put a burr under her saddle. I can't picture Raquel acting like that. Can you?"

Fudge's breathing had become lighter and the weight of his head on her shoulder heavier. She checked and sure enough, his eyes were closed. In all the years they'd been together, she'd never seen him more at peace.

"I don't know what to do, Fudgie."

His ears flicked back. He wasn't completely asleep.

"We've been going along just fine, you and me. We know that works. We don't know if this new thing would work." Sliding gently away from him, she stood back and took a deep breath. "What do you think?"

He regarded her solemnly.

"You're not going to tell me what to do, either, are you?"

Damned if he didn't shake his head. Probably a fly made him do it, but who knew for sure? She smiled. "Alrighty, then. Thanks for trusting me to make the right decision... for everyone."

<u>37</u>

How long would he have to wait? Luis paced barefoot through the casita, the cool tile relieving the hot soles of his tender feet. Occasionally he paused to stare out the front window in case he might catch a glimpse of Jordan heading his way.

He'd stopped expecting a call after his addled brain coughed up the info that her phone was likely in her backpack. Chances were slim she'd paused mid-flight to grab the backpack out of his truck.

That would have slowed her down. He'd spooked her bad. He still marveled at the speed she'd generated. And wearing boots, no less.

Now that she'd made her escape, she might not come out of hiding for hours. Served him right. Cole had promised to talk to her, but Cole wasn't exactly on his side.

Nor should he be. In Cole's shoes, he'd be protective as hell, too.

As the minutes ticked by, he endlessly played the *what if* game. What if he'd kept his big mouth shut? What if he'd let the decision percolate while he wooed her with an intimate dinner and more lovemaking?

Or even better, what if he'd taken her on a sunset ride around the ranch, giving her a private tour to precede tomorrow's formal one? They might have come across a few of the herds, maybe even spotted her adoptees.

What if he'd bided his time, waiting for the perfect moment to reintroduce Mila's idea? What if he'd led up to it gradually instead of hitting her with it like a cream pie in the face? What if—

His phone chimed with the generic ring he used for all calls other than his family members. It could be anyone. Or it could be….

He grabbed his phone. *Jordan.* His heart beat so fast he couldn't breathe. He tapped it and gulped. "Hi."

"It's crazy. I promised I would never call you and here I am doing it again."

He closed his eyes. "Why?"

"Cole told you I'd be in touch. You said I could call or text."

"But your phone is…." Or was. Just because she had it now didn't mean she was nearby. She could have quietly snuck into his cab and retrieved her backpack. She could be back inside her trailer.

Or right outside his door.

He approached it slowly, bracing himself for disappointment. "I appreciate the call."

"I thought you might." She sounded breathless. "You said you liked hearing my voice in your ear."

"I do." His hand trembled as he reached for the wrought iron handle. "But I also like looking at you." He opened the door.

"How convenient." She lowered the phone and tucked it in the backpack over her shoulder. "Here I am."

Words deserted him. She looked the same, but different. The sun was behind her, surrounding her with light, making her golden hair glow. She looked like an angel.

"Can I come in?"

"Yes. Yes, come in." He stepped back and almost tripped over his own sore feet. "Can I get you a drink? Iced tea? Lemonade? A beer? Or—"

"Thanks, but... could we just talk?"

"Sure." His stomach in a knot, he closed the door and tried unsuccessfully to tuck his phone in his back pocket. Finally he gave up and laid it on the small table by the door where he kept his keys.

She unhooked her backpack. "Would you please put that over there, too?"

"Sure." Great vocabulary he had going on.

"Okay." She swallowed. "Here goes. I've given this thing a lot of thought and I think it might work, but there are a couple of details we should iron—"

"This thing?" He stared at her. "Do you mean—"

"You and me."

The breath left his lungs. "*Dios mio.*" It came out a whisper and he began to shake.

She moved closer. "That's why I'm here. I figured you'd know—"

"But I screwed everything up."

"You did." She rested her hands on his chest. "But your heart's in the right place."

"And now it's beating so fast I can't think." He cleared his throat. "What... what details?"

"I'm hoping we could set up a fifty-fifty split between time on the road and time here."

"You'd be fine with staying here half the time?" He took hold of her waist just to steady himself. And to confirm this was real. That she was real. And talking about a potential future.

Light flared in her eyes. "I love you." Sliding her hands up his chest, she gripped his shoulders. "I don't want to spend half the year away from you and I also want you to be able to do your work. I'd enjoy seeing you do it. Maybe I could help out now and then."

"That would be great." *She loved him.* He'd told Monty that she did, but had he truly believed it himself? He did now. There was no doubting the intensity in her gaze. Not only did she love him, she wanted a life with him.

But unlike his wild leap of faith this afternoon, she was approaching the prospect with care. Gradually, like the sun sliding over the horizon at dawn and slowly illuminating the landscape, she was showing him the future he'd dreamed of.

But he was wiser, now. "You love your work, too. And traveling."

"I have a feeling that traveling solo might not be much fun anymore."

"Oh?" That was good news.

"But I'd like to offer clinics here when we're not on the road. Do you think your family—"

"Yes."

"You don't need to check with them?"

"No. Having a trainer of your caliber on board is a net positive."

She blinked. "I'm a net positive?"

"Yes, ma'am." Warmth in his chest began to spread. "For the ranch. And me."

"Well, then." Her breath hitched. "I… um… would like to keep Sterling as my legal name because it's my brand."

He skipped right over the branding thing to the heart of the matter. "Are you talking about getting married?"

"Of course! I know you want to."

"I do." He tamped down the bubbles of joy. He'd learned the hard way to pay attention, and *I know you want to* wasn't good enough. "Do *you* want to get married?"

She met his gaze, her expression radiant. "Yes, I do. Very much."

He turned loose the bubbles. "I love you. I love you so much. I—"

"The name thing isn't a deal breaker?"

"Hell, no."

"Our kids should be Bridgers, though."

"Babies, too?" He tucked her in close. If he didn't stay anchored he might start floating.

"I've had daydreams about having kids. That's why I bought the Ranch Puppy series. But I figured I'd always be missing a big part of that picture."

He smiled. "Are you saying I might belong in that empty space?"

"Kinda looks that way, doesn't it?"

He sent a prayer of thanks heavenward. "It does, *querida.*" Lowering his head, he savored the moment right before his lips touched hers. Her soft sigh of happiness told him all he needed to know.

The passion they'd shared years ago had deepened into love. And as he kissed her, he tasted something more, something he'd begun to think he'd never find... the sweet promise of forever.

* * * * *

For Cole Sterling, Christmas is a holiday to avoid, but the Bridger Bunch has other plans in WHEN A COWBOY SKIPS CHRISTMAS, book three of the Bridger Bunch series!

* * * * *